Kuno Fischer, Ellen Frothingham, Henry Holt, Gotthold Ephraim
Lessing

Nathan the Wise

A Dramatic Poem

Kuno Fischer, Ellen Frothingham, Henry Holt, Gotthold Ephraim Lessing

Nathan the Wise
A Dramatic Poem

ISBN/EAN: 9783337376642

Printed in Europe, USA, Canada, Australia, Japan

Cover: Foto ©Andreas Hilbeck / pixelio.de

More available books at **www.hansebooks.com**

Nathan the Wise

A Dramatic Poem by

Gotthold Ephraim Lessing

Translated by

Ellen Frothingham

*Preceded by a brief account of the Poet and his works,
and followed by Kuno Fischer's
Essay on the Poem*

THIRD EDITION, REVISED

NEW YORK

HENRY HOLT AND COMPANY

1873.

Publishers' Notice

To the First Edition.

Nathan the Wise is the third of a uniform series of great foreign poems which the publishers have lately begun to issue. The first one was King René's Daughter, from the Danish, which is now in the second edition. It was followed by Frithiof's Saga, the national epic of Sweden, edited by Bayard Taylor. The fourth of the series, Selections from the Kalevala, the national epic of Finland, translated from a close German version by the late Professor John A. Porter, of Yale College, will be ready for publication a few days after the issue of the present volume. Others will be added as rapidly as the public appreciation may warrant. Among those in contemplation are Calderon's Life is a Dream; Tasso's Aminta, translated by Leigh Hunt; The Wooing of the King's Daughter, from the Norwegian of Muench; Boris Godounoff, from the Russian of Pouschkine; Nala and Damajanti,

translated from the Sanscrit by Milman; a translation of Bodenstedt's version of the Turkish songs
of Mirza Schaffy, and an English version of the
Sakoontalá.

With the exception of Goethe's FAUST, there is no
poem in German literature which has received so
much special study as NATHAN THE WISE, or which
has so well rewarded it. Probably the best critical
monograph which it has generated is the essay by
Kuno Fischer. This has been translated by the
translator of the poem, pruned of some of its German redundancy, and put into a form better suited
than the original one, to the Anglo-Saxon requirements of terseness and directness. The modified
version will be found at the end of this volume.

Sketch of Lessing.

" If God held all truth shut in his right hand,
and in his left nothing but the ever-restless instinct
for truth, though with the condition of for ever
and ever erring, and should say to me, Choose! I
would bow reverently to his left hand, and say,
Father, give! Pure truth is for Thee alone!"

Two years ago, it would have been safe to say
that a vague recollection of having somewhere seen
a sentence like the one we have quoted, was all the
knowledge of Gotthold Ephraim Lessing possessed
by the majority of educated Americans. Of course
there are men who have long known and appreciated him ; but the number of such is surprisingly
small. He has not had one reader where Goethe,
or Schiller, or Jean Paul, has had a hundred. The
only one of his works yet published in this country
is Minna von Barnhelm—surely not his most characteristic production—and this was reprinted by a

publisher of school-books from an English edition
adapted for the use of students of German.   It is
but a year since Mr. Spencer published Professor
Evans' excellent translation of Stahr's Life of Lessing.   The 'criticisms' which the volume received,
clearly displayed the ignorance existing in regard to
its subject.   Among the few notable exceptions were
a short notice in the *Nation*, and an article in the
North American Review for April, 1867, by Professor
Lowell, in which he gave an admirable sketch of
Lessing's life and character.   A 'Review,' published in New York, contained an 'essay,' the first
half of which was translated from the *Nouvelle Bio-
graphie Générale*, and the other half taken from Ap-
pleton's *Cyclopædia*.   As far as we have been able to
learn, the American press has supplied little more
than these meagre materials for a knowledge of that
great and unique man.

The neglect that he has received cannot be accounted for by any proportionate inferiority to his
better known countrymen.   He was the generator
of modern German literature, and it is not on the
partly accidental position of a pioneer that his
claims rest.   He had a greatness of his own, whose
half prophetic character does much to explain
the neglect which has fallen upon it.   The hack-
neyed term, "in advance of his age," has a very
deep significance when applied to him.   But we are
beginning to catch up with him, and the peculiar

progress of our people has already made them specially fitted for his teachings.

For a knowledge of the poet and his other works, we recommend the sources already named. We have gleaned from them, for the benefit of readers unwise enough to slight this recommendation, the facts embodied in the following sketch.

On the 22d of January, 1729, Deacon, afterward Pastor Primarius, John Gottfried Lessing, of Kamenz, in Upper Lusatia, rejoiced, it is to be supposed, over the birth of his eldest son. The little Lessing began life with a line of ancestors at his back who, through scholarly attainments and liberal ideas, legitimately gave him the power which afterward made him great. For half-a-dozen generations, his family had been one of jurists, curates, and burgomasters. His grandfather's thesis, on taking his degree of Doctor of Laws, was, "*De Religionum Tolerantia.*" Added to the boy's other 'inherited conditions,' was a fine physical constitution.

When Lessing was about twelve years old, the rector of the Kamenz public school, where Lessing went, published an article defending the theme that "The Stage is a School of Eloquence." This brought all the big-wigs of the town down upon him. Pastor Primarius Lessing assailed his principles in the pulpit, and at last he had to leave the place. A friend of his—Mylius by name, whom

we shall meet again—wrote a satirical poem on
the circumstance, in consequence of which he was
imprisoned, forced to apologize, and fined. This
affair probably presented the Stage for the first
time to the notice of the future founder of the
German drama. The immediate effect was, that
he had to go to another school—that of St. Afra,
established by the Elector Maurice of Saxony, in
Meissen. On the 21st of June, 1841, a festival was
held at that same school, in honor of the cen-
tennial anniversary of Lessing's entrance. The old
pastor took him there to have him prepared for the
ministry. After Lessing left, he said that he had
"already at Meissen understood how one must learn
much there which one cannot use in the world."
That was more than a hundred years ago. Perhaps
schools have changed since then. At Meissen,
Lessing's favorite authors were Theophrastus, Plau-
tus, and Terence, and he said that he got self-
knowledge by reading "comedies." At this school
he wrote parts of a poem "On the Plurality of
Worlds." One expression in it is—"They make
glorious shipwreck who are lost in seeking worlds."
He also began his first dramatic work—a comedy—
"The Young Scholar," of which he says that at
that time, when he "knew men only from books,
a young scholar was the only species of fool" which
he could not have been unacquainted with.

In September, 1746, when he was seventeen years

old, he entered the University of Leipzic. While there, he studied the literature of the ancients with an interest far removed from the pedantic study of their languages then in vogue. He was also one of a little coterie who talked philosophy with Kaestner, a young professor of great talent and enthusiasm. The world of Leipzic made Lessing realize, as he wrote to his mother, that "books might make him learned, but would never make him a man." He felt himself pedantic, awkward, and boorish; and in order to correct these defects, learned dancing, fencing, and riding, and sought society. The theatre at once attracted him. He became acquainted with Madame Neuber, the head of the dramatic company—a woman who, Lessing says, "had manly views, and a perfect knowledge of her art." Meanwhile, he had fallen in with Mylius, the youth who got put in prison for his poem, who became a strong influence in directing the course of Lessing's life. Mylius was now one of the little philosophical coterie gathered about Professor Kaestner; he was a man of great talent, very unorthodox opinions, and irregular life. He published popular journals on scientific subjects, for which Lessing occasionally wrote poetic burlesques of scientific discussions. This man led Lessing more among the stage-people, and Lessing, of course, fell in love, very platonically, we are assured, with one of the young actresses. These associations led him to

finish "The Young Scholar," and it was played
with great success by Madame Neuber's company.

It is not much to the discredit of the poor old
Pastor Primarius that, in an age when actors were
considered too vile for Christian burial, he thought
that, in such company, his son was going to per-
dition. He pretended that Lessing's mother was
dying, and sent for him to come to her. A heavy
frost set in after the mailing of the letter, and Lessing started without waiting for winter clothing.
The parents were softened when their boy stood
before them shivering with the severe cold, and he
was made welcome. After three months, he went
back to college. His parents considering that he
had dwelt so long in the tents of the ungodly that
it would be a desecration of the priestly office for
him to embrace it, tried to make him a student of
medicine. He yielded so far as to attend several
courses of medical lectures.

Madame Neuber's theatre was soon broken up,
and Lessing had gone security for so many of the
debts of the actors, that, as no help could be looked
for from home, he was obliged to leave Leipzic. Going to Berlin, where Mylius was already
editing a paper, he concluded to abandon study,
and to try to relieve himself from his debts with
his pen.

Mylius did all he could for his friend, not stop-
ping short at real sacrifices. But the influence of

"the free-thinker" was greatly dreaded by the good
people at Kamenz, and they were further exercised
by frequent rumors of their son's predilection for
the stage. Their letters were full of urging to leave
Berlin, and complaints at his course of life and
irreligious opinions. A few sentences from his replies will throw light on some points in his character. "I shall not return home, neither shall I go
to any university; because my stipends" (allow-
ances made by his native town for the support of a
few of its young men at a university) "are not suffi-
cient to pay my debts, and I cannot ask the necessary sum of you. . . . Wherever I may be, I
shall continue to write, and I shall never forget the
benefits I have so long received at your hands.
. . . *The Christian religion is not a thing that
ought to be received on trust from one's parents.* The
great mass of mankind, it is true, inherit it as they
do their property; but their conduct shows what
Christians they are." The ideas in this latter para-
graph are common-place enough now, but Lessing
wrote them in Germany a hundred and twenty years
ago, when he was twenty years old.

With the exception of part of 1752, spent in Wit-
tenberg in studying for his degree of Master of
Arts, the next ten years were mainly passed in
Berlin.

Lessing began work in Berlin by making trans-
lations from the modern languages. He knew

French, Spanish, Italian, and English. Soon he
founded, in connection with Mylius, a periodical
devoted to dramatic subjects, ancient as well as
modern. He withdrew from this publication because Mylius was ignorant enough to assert in it
that there had been no Italian drama. He then
began writing for Voss's *Gazette.* By this time he
began to attract attention. German criticism was
divided between the followers of Gottsched, who in-
sisted on exact imitation in form and fact, and the
Zurich school, who set no bounds to the imagination. Lessing struck out a new path, by declaring
that there are no *a priori* principles in art, that the
only established canons are those that can be in-
duced from works of art already existing, and that a
fresh genius gives material for fresh canons. In
other words, he applied to art the 'experience'
principle of philosophy. He began hitting hard
blows at the pedantry as well as the sentimentalism
of the time, and directed them particularly against
the French influence which was spreading both.
The French classic drama was the model in Germany, and it was believed that classic themes were
the only ones for tragedy. Lessing's English culture
showed him so many illustrations of the falsity of
this view, that he hunted out the principles which
prove that man at one time is as much a subject
for art as at another—that the soul of man, and not
his surroundings, is the seat of all that is great in

dramatic poetry. In illustration of his realistic principles, he wrote, in 1753–5, "Miss Sara Sampson" —a tragedy in prose, the scene laid in England, and the time contemporaneous. The play was a success, and emancipated the German playwrights from their previous limitations.

Carrying the same disregard of precedent and the same adherence to broad principles, into religion, he began quite early in his Berlin career to strike out such thoughts as these: "Well-doing is the main thing: belief is secondary." . . . "It is not agreement in opinions, but agreement in virtuous actions, that renders the world virtuous and happy." Of a romance whose scene was laid in Constantinople, he said: "If a pious Moslem should read the book, he would constantly be constrained to cry out, 'What blasphemies!' and yet it is these very blasphemies which will edify many an honest Christian." Nor did his religious views stop short of self-application. He carried about in his poverty a calm, cheerful philosophy, which prevented his believing that "one should thank God only for good things," and led him to believe that in man "it does not concern his conscience how useful he is, but how useful he would be." Lessing further carried out his healthy ideas against the licentiousness creeping into literature from the French influence. The central point of his theories of success in art was the character of the artist. To one trying to write for the stage, he says, "Study ethics, . . . cultivate your own character."

His mode of life during these years must be judged with reference to the current views of the age. He was temperately fond of his wine-cellar, as the most sedate Germans are to-day, but he gambled a great deal harder than present ideas approve. He continued this practice for many years, and said that "the eager attention which he gave the faro-table set his clogged machine in motion— brought the stagnant juices into circulation." There is no evidence that he gambled for gain, and all his views and generous habits forbid such a supposition.

He had not been in Berlin long before he began to make valuable friendships. Among the best and most enduring were those with Nicolai and Moses Mendelssohn—the grandfather of Felix. The friendship with Mendelssohn was life-long, and naturally has given rise to the notion that in Nathan the Wise, Lessing intended to portray his Jewish friend. Not only was he honored in these great friends, but was likewise honored in a still greater enemy—Voltaire. The acrid philosopher was then engaged in his disgraceful lawsuit with Hirsch, and employed Lessing to translate some of the papers into German. This drew Lessing into Voltaire's society daily for some time. Lessing learned how to appreciate him ; but he was not the man to appreciate Lessing :

and when Lessing borrowed from his secretary the manuscript of the newly completed *Siècle de Louis XIV.*, Voltaire finding it out, feared some translating and reprinting plot. He wrote two insulting letters to Lessing, and received the replies he merited. This little affair naturally did not tend to soften the criticism which Lessing always felt it his duty to give Voltaire's imaginative writings, but it can hardly be regretted if it had any influence in inspiring what sometimes seems the best *bon mot* in all literature. Nicolai once said to Lessing, "You must admit that Voltaire has lately said many new and good things." "Certainly," answered Lessing, "but the new things are not good, and the good things are not new."

In 1760, Lessing was driven by his poverty to accept a position as assistant of General Von Tauenzien, the director of Frederic's Mint at Breslau. Up to this time, his writings had consisted almost entirely of special criticisms and polemic letters. His only other works had been his *Fabeln*, the beautiful little tragedy of Philotas, and two dramas on the subject of Faust—one of which is lost, and the other exists but in fragments. At Breslau he remained five years. He was in comparative prosperity, though not as great as it might have been had he not used his knowledge of the mint operations most conscientiously. His peace of mind had two drawbacks—his family, who made the most shameless demands on his finances, which he was too tender-hearted to treat wisely; and his Berlin friends, who bewailed his absence from them as a waste of time, and said that without him they could not continue the "Letters on Literature," which had been the most important vehicles of German criticism. His life seems to have been full of diversion and full of work. Goethe says that Lessing "was fond of casting off personal dignity, because he was confident that he could resume it at any time; and delighted at that period to lead a dissipated life in taverns and society, since he needed constantly a strong counterpoise to his powerfully laborious soul." The fact that his soul was "powerfully laborious" during the Breslau period, is proven by the production of the first works that support his enduring fame—Minna von Barnhelm—a military drama, founded on his army associations, among which had been his presence at the siege of Schweidnitz, and the Laokoön—one of the greatest systematic treatises on art criticism in existence.

During the summer of 1764, when he was thirty-five years old, Lessing broke down into an inflammatory fever. It was his first hard sickness. When convalescing, he wrote: "I hope that this will soon pass away, and then I shall be as new-born. All changes of our temperament, I believe, are connected with the processes of our animal economy. The crisis of my life approaches; I begin to be a man, and flatter myself that in this burning fever I have ıaved away the last trace of my youthful follies. . . You wish me to be healthy; but ought poets to wish for robust health? The Horaces dwell in feeble bodies, the healthy Lessings become game-sters and tipplers. Yet wish me healthy, dear friend; but, if possible, healthy with a slight memento, a thorn in the flesh, which shall make the poet feel from time to time the frailty of the man."

The next year Lessing returned to Berlin, bringing with him nothing but a library, which he afteıward sold at a great sacrifice. He fought poverty with his pen for a couple of years, was disappointed in an effort to get the place of royal librarian from Frederic, and in 1767 accepted the position of theatre director at Hamburg. This led to his writ-ing a series of dramatic essays, preserved under the title of *Dramaturgie.* Its position among works of dramatic criticism is not unworthy of comparison ,ith the place which the Laokoön occupies in rela-tion to art in general. At the close of the *Drama-turgie* he expresses the following interesting estimate of his own powers : "I am neither actor nor poet. . . . I do not feel in myself the living fountain which lifts itself by its own strength, and by its own strength sports and spreads in radiations so rich, so fresh, so pure! With me it is all squeezing and pumping! I should be altogether poor, and cold, and short-sighted, did I not know how to borrow occasionally, with discretion, from foreign treasures, to warm myself at another man's fire, and to strengthen my sight with the optic glasses of art. I have, therefore, always been ashamed and angry when I have heard or read anything derogatory to criticism. Criticism, it is said, stifles genius; whereas I flatter myself that I have received from it something that comes very near to genius." Yet, Goethe said, "Lessing wished to disclaim the title of poet, but his immortal works testify against himself."

The author of the *Dramaturgie* found it impossible to keep peace in the theatrical camp while he indulged in special criticism; and after he had expressed his views on the general principles of dramatic art, there was no further practicable field for his efforts. A publishing enterprise, into which he had gone, failed, and left him in debt. His works were bringing him nothing; in no small degree because they could be reprinted and re-acted in every petty province of Germany without the author receiving any reward; for the German nations were no nearer a civilized position regarding international copyright, a hundred years ago, than the United States of America are to-day.

Relief, however, seemed at hand. Frederick William Ferdinand, Duke of Brunswick, a literary toady, heard that such an ornamental appendage to his court as Lessing would make, could be had cheap, and offered him the positon of librarian at Wolfenbüttel, at a very modest salary. Lessing was now about forty years old, and his poverty was the more irksome because he wished to marry. In Hamburg, he was a favored friend in the family of a certain König, and there is reason to believe that he had to smother a feeling toward his friend's wife, which, as it appeared hopeless, made him desirous of leaving the city. But his friend König died in 1769, and within a reasonable time Lessing and Eva König were engaged. These circumstances made him ready to accept a fixed occupation, even to the prejudice of his literary pursuits, and he accepted the duke's offer.

The residence at Wolfenbüttel occupied six years that were anything but happy. The place was unhealthy, he had no congenial society, was liable to interruption at all times, had to do an immense amount of purely routine work, and was constantly sick at heart from hope deferred. The letters passing between him and Eva are full of the most beautiful sincerity, unselfishness, and common sense regarding all matters of the intellect and emotions ; but they are not the letters of people possessing a healthy capacity for cutting the gordian knots of circumstances.

König's affairs were left in such a complicated condition that it was hard to settle his estate for the best advantage of his wife and four children, and

Eva felt that she ought not to marry while the finances of the little ones were in such an uncertain condition. Lessing, on his part, had little more to depend upon than the illusive promises by which the Duke kept him in his place.

Six years wore away in separation and anxious uncertainty. As may be imagined, they were not very productive years for Lessing. During them he gave to the world the "Wolfenbüttel Fragments," which led to the controversy with Götze. This affair is described in the essay at the end of this volume. He also finished *Emilia Galotti*,* a tragedy that he had begun fifteen years before, while he was warm with enthusiasm for the regeneration of dramatic art. The motive of this tragedy is that of Virginius applied to modern circumstances. In dramatic merit, it is Lessing's best production, and it is at the same time a consistent embodiment and beautiful illustration of those principles of dramatic art, of which, considering his time and circumstances, he may be called a creator.

In 1775, Lessing went into Italy with the crown-prince of Brunswick, and was received everywhere with great attention. In Vienna, *Emilia Galotti* was played, and the poet was received with an ovation. Maria Theresa sent for him, and sought his opinions regarding the intellectual development of the

---

* Now while we write, this play, in the original German, is on the programme of the leading theatre in New York.

empire. At Rome, he was presented to the Pope, and treated by the dignitaries in a manner which contrasted honorably with his treatment by eminent persons at home.

In 1776, he returned to Wolfenbüttel, and he and Eva were married. She was worthy of him, and he seemed entering on a new career of usefulness and happiness. In a year a son was born, but he lived only a day, and his mother died a few days after. This is the first overwhelming sorrow we know of in Lessing's life. To our mind, nothing in all the letters he wrote at the time reveals its intensity so much as this: "I was so sorry to lose him, this son, for he had so much sense ! so much sense ! Do not think that my few hours of fatherhood have already made me such an ape of a father ! I know what I say ! Did it not show his sense that they were obliged to draw him into the world with forceps? that he so soon became disgusted with his new abode? Was he not wise in seizing the first opportunity to make off again?" We hope that not many of our readers know what this tendency to turn one's own sorrow into a jest means. Shakspeare knew it : if he did not, he could not have written this strange passage in Hamlet :

Ghost [*beneath*]. Swear !
Hamlet. Ah, ha, boy ! say'st thou so ? Art thou there, truepenny ?
*   *   *   *   *   *   *
Ghost [*beneath*]. Swear !
Hamlet. Well said, old mole ! Canst work i' th' ground so fast ?

The death of Lessing's wife re-made him. There-
after, the dominant passion in his heart was not
criticism, but sympathy. But he was dragged into
controversy, and he had not lost the old heroic
nature which made him, early in life, say that he
never was at his best unless against an antagonist.
Yet his fighting, and nearly all else that he did,
was directly intended to promote the spiritual and
moral progress of mankind. He devoted himself
more to the profound questions of philosophy, and
seems to have reached that plane of thought and
interests which lies at the foundation of all other
human effort. But little more than three years were
left him. They were full of loneliness, though not
from lack of friends, and of privation and weariness.
Here are a few passages in one of his letters to
Eliza Reimarus : "I must pay dearly for a single
year that I lived with a rational woman. I must
sacrifice all, all, in order not to expose myself to a
suspicion which is utterly intolerable to me." In
this, he alluded to his having again gone into debt
for the sake of securing his wife's property to her
children. "How often," he continues, "do I feel
tempted to curse the day when I even once wished
to be as happy as other people!" . . . "Yet I am
too proud to acknowledge myself unhappy—only
set the teeth, and let the boat drift at the mercy of
the winds and waves. Enough that I will not upset
it myself." But to the outer world, he was very calm

and strong. While these great forces were tugging at his soul, he produced "Nathan the Wise"—a poem worthy of such a birth, and probably impossible without it. During these last years, he also wrote the "Five Conversations, for Freemasons," in which he expressed his ideas of government and society, and "The Education of the Human Race," in which he stated his views of religious development. The first of the three is here to speak for itself. The other two are full of pregnant ideas, and, indeed, the very title of the latter was considered a happy embodiment of suggestive thought when it reappeared, a few years since, in "Essays and Reviews."

Lessing died while on a visit to Brunswick, on the fifteenth of February, 1781. The newspapers in Hamburg were forbidden to publish anything in his praise, and the clergy endeavored to prevent a public ceremony in honor of his memory. Thus he shared the fate which, so far, has been appointed for the great Teachers. While it cannot be claimed that his labors are to be classed with those of the few men who are universally honored as finders of fundamental truths, the attainments he did make, after having forced his path through the errors of a strangely artificial and distorted age, give room to believe that had he been left to live a rounded life, he would have placed himself among those who are remembered not only always, but everywhere.

H. H.

NATHAN THE WISE.

DRAMATIS PERSONÆ.

SULTAN SALADIN.

SITTAH, his Sister.

NATHAN, a rich Jew of Jerusalem.

RECHA, his adopted Daughter.

DAJA, a Christian woman, living in the Jew's house as Recha's companion.

A Young Templar.

A Dervise.

The Patriarch of Jerusalem.

A Lay-Brother.

An Emir.

Mamelukes in Saladin's service.

The scene is in Jerusalem.

ACT FIRST.

Scene I.

Hall in Nathan's House.

Nathan *returning from a journey.* Daja *meeting him.*

Daja.

'Tis he; 'tis Nathan! God be ever praised
That you're returned to us again at last!

Nathan.

Ay, Daja; God be praised! But why "at last?"
Was it my purpose to have come before?
Could I have come before? for Babylon
Is from Jerusalem, as I was forced
To travel, turning oft to right and left,
A good two hundred leagues. Collecting debts,
Besides, is not a work to be dispatched
In haste, or easily turned off.

Daja.

                  Oh, Nathan,
What misery, what misery meanwhile
Might have befallen you here! Your house—

NATHAN.

Took fire,
That have I heard already. God but grant
I've heard the whole!

DAJA.

And might have easily
Been leveled with the ground.

NATHAN.

Then had we built
Another and a better.

DAJA.

True; but Recha,
Within a hair's breadth was she burned to death.

NATHAN.

Burned!—who?—my Recha? That I had not
heard.
Why, then, a house I should no more have needed.
Within a hair's breadth burned to death! She *was*—
Was burned to death! Speak out—speak out, I say!
Slay me and torture me no longer! Yes,
She has been burned to death!

DAJA.

And if she were,
Should I be telling it?

NATHAN.

Why fright me then?
O Recha! O my Recha!

DAJA.

Yours—your Recha?

NATHAN.

God grant I ne'er may have to unlearn the use
Of calling her my child!

DAJA.

And call you all
That you possess, with equal right your own?

NATHAN.

Naught with a greater. All I else possess
Has been bestowed by Nature and by Fortune.
This is the only gift I owe to Virtue.

DAJA.

O Nathan, what a price you make me pay
For all your kindness! if aught exercised
From such a motive can be called a kindness.

NATHAN.

From such a motive? What?

DAJA.

My conscience—

NATHAN.

Daja,

Let me but tell you first—

DAJA.

I say my conscience—

1*

NATHAN.

What stuffs in Babylon I bought for you !
So precious and so tasteful.   Recha's own
Are scarcely fairer.

DAJA.

All in vain.   My conscience,
I tell you, will no more be lulled to sleep.

NATHAN.

And how you will delight in all the jewels,
The rings, the clasps, the ear-rings, and the chains,
That in Damascus I selected for you,
I'm eager to behold.

DAJA.

How like yourself !
You must be always giving, always giving.

NATHAN.

Take gladly, as I give you, and—be silent !

DAJA.

Be silent !   Doubts there any one that Nathan
Is honor, generosity itself ?
And yet—

NATHAN.

I'm but a Jew.   Is that your meaning ?

DAJA.

You know my meaning better.

NATHAN.

Then be silent.

DAJA.

I will be silent. What of guilt grow hence
In sight of God, which I cannot prevent,
I cannot change—cannot,—fall on your head.

NATHAN.

Fall on my head! But tell me where she is.
Where tarries she? Ah, should you have deceived
    me!
Knows she I'm here?

DAJA.

    I might retort the question.
Her every nerve still trembles with affright.
Her fancy colors with a glow of fire
Whate'er it paints. In sleep her spirit wakes;
Awake, it sleeps: inferior now to brutes,
Superior now to angels.

NATHAN.

    Ah, poor child!
What are we men!

DAJA.

    This morning long she lay,
With eyelids closed, as she were dead. Then quick
Sprang up, cried, "Hark, my father's camels come!
Hark, his own gentle voice!" Then drooped again
Her eyelids, and, the arm's support withdrawn,

Her head once more fell back upon the pillows.
I hasted through the gate, and, lo ! 'twas you—
'Twas you, indeed, approaching ! And what won-
    der?
For her whole soul has since been but with you—
And him.

NATHAN.

    And him ! What him ?

DAJA.

                 Who from the fire
Preserved her.

NATHAN.

        Who was that? Where is he now?
Who was it that preserved my Recha for me?

DAJA.

A Templar, who, some days before a prisoner,
Was hither brought, and pardoned by the Sultan.

NATHAN.

A Templar granted life by Saladin?
Could no less miracle have saved my Recha?
God !

DAJA.

    But for him who boldly risked again
His unexpected boon, she had been lost.

NATHAN.

Where is this noble man ? Where is he, Daja ?

Conduct me to his feet. Whatever treasure
Was left you, you bestowed on him at once ;
Gave all ; with promises of more—much more ?

DAJA.

How could we ?

NATHAN.

Did you not ?

DAJA.

He came, but whence
None knew ; he went, and whither none could tell.
A stranger to the house, his ear alone
To guide him, onward through the smoke and
   flame,
With outstretched mantle, fearlessly he pressed
Toward the voice that cried to us for help.
Already had we given him up for lost,
When suddenly, from out the smoke and flame,
He stood before us, bearing her aloft
In his strong arms. By our exultant thanks
Unmoved, he laid his burden on the ground,
Pressed through the multitude his way, and vanished.

NATHAN.

But not, I hope, forever.

DAJA.

Many days
We saw him yonder, walking to and fro
Beneath the palms that shade the sepulchre

Of our ascended Lord.   I went to him
With rapture; thanked him, praised, commanded,
    begged
He would but once behold the grateful girl,
Who could not rest till at her savior's feet
She'd wept her thanks.

NATHAN.

Well?

DAJA.

             Useless ; he was deaf
To our entreaties, and he poured, besides,
Such scorn upon me—

NATHAN.

        You were frightened off.

DAJA.

Nay; anything but that.   Day after day
I went to him again ; day after day
Let him again insult me.   There is nothing
I've not endured from him ; nothing that gladly
I'd not have still endured.   But long he's ceased
To walk beneath the palms that shade the grave
Of our ascended Lord, and no one knows
His dwelling-place.—You are amazed ; you pon-
    der?

NATHAN.

I ponder the effect this must produce
Upon a mind like Recha's.   To be scorned

By one whom she is bound to prize so highly :
'To be at once repelled and yet attracted.
'Twixt head and heart long contest must ensue,
If sorrow or misanthropy shall conquer.
)ft neither triumphs, and imagination
Becoming party in the strife, creates
A dreamer, in whom now the head usurps
The place of heart, and now the heart plays head.
Sad interchange !   If I mistake not Recha,
The latter is her fate.   She yields to fancies.

DAJA.

But then so pure, so lovely !

NATHAN.
Fancies still.

DAJA.

Above the rest, one—fancy, if you will—
She cherishes.   Her Templar, as she deems,
Is not a mortal being, not of earth.
One of the angels, to whose guardian care,
Her little heart from childhood fondly thought
Itself intrusted, stepped from out the cloud
Beneath whose veil he hitherto had hovered
About her even in the fire, and stood
Revealed as Templar.—Do not smile !   Who knows?
At least, if smile you must, do not destroy
A fancy shared alike by Christian, Jew,
And Mussulman,—so beautiful a fancy.

NATHAN.

And beautiful to me.—Go, trusty Daja,
See how she is—if I may speak with her.
Then I will seek this freakish guardian angel;
And if it be his pleasure still to dwell
Among us on the earth, and wear the guise
Of so unmannerly a knight, doubt not
I shall discover and conduct him hither.

DAJA.

You promise much.

NATHAN.

      Should then this sweet conceit
Be changed to sweeter truth—for, trust me, Daja,
To human heart more dear is man than angel—
You'll surely not with me—with me—be vexed
If so this angel-dreamer shall be cured.

DAJA.

How good you are, and yet how bad withal!
I go.   But hark! but see!   She comes herself.

SCENE II.

RECHA *and the preceding.*

RECHA.

Is it in very truth yourself, my father?
I thought you had but sent your voice before.

Where tarry you? What deserts or what moun-
tains,
What rivers, separate us now? We breathe
Beneath one roof, and yet you hasten not.
To clasp your Recha, who was burned meanwhile!
Poor Recha! Almost, only almost burned.
Nay, shudder not! Oh, 'tis an ugly death
To die by fire!

NATHAN.

My child! my darling child!

RECHA.

You had to cross the Euphrates, Tigris, Jordan,—
Who knows how many more? Oft for your life
I trembled till the fire enveloped me;
But since the fire enveloped me, to die
By water seems refreshment, solace, balm.
But you have not been drowned, nor I been burned.
We will rejoice, and give God thanks. He bore
Your boat and you upon the unseen wings
Of angels over all the faithless streams:
He bade my angel visibly unfold
His snowy wings, and bear me through the fire.

NATHAN.

(His snowy wings! Ah, yes; the Templar's mantle,
Outstretched and white.)

RECHA.

Ay; visibly to bear me

From out the flames, fanned backward by his wings.
Thus have I seen an angel face to face—
My guardian-angel.

NATHAN.

Recha would be worth
An angel's visiting, and would in him
See naught more fair than he in her.

RECHA (*smiling*).

My father,
Whom flatter you—the angel or yourself?

NATHAN.

Had but a human being, such a man
As Nature daily grants, this service rendered,
He must for you have been an angel; ay,
He must and would.

RECHA.

Not such an angel.   No;
This was in truth, in very truth an angel.
Have you yourself not taught me to believe
That angels are; that God for them that love Him
Can yet work miracles?   I love Him.

NATHAN.

Yes;
And He loves you; and hourly miracles
For you, and such as you, is working now;
From all eternity has worked them for you.

RECHA.

I love to hear it.

NATHAN.

Natural it sounds
And commonplace to have a Templar save you ;
But is it therefore less a miracle ?
The greatest miracle of all is this :
That-true and genuine miracles become
Of no significance.   Without that wonder
Scarce would a thoughtful man bestow the name
On things that only children should admire,
Who, gaping, follow what is new and strange.

DAJA (*to Nathan*).

Would you to bursting strain her o'erwrought brain
With all your subtleties ?

NATHAN.

Trust her to me !
Were it not miracle enough for Recha
To be delivered by a human being,
Himself by no small miracle first saved ?
Not small indeed !   Who ever heard before
Of Templar being spared by Saladin—
Of Templar asking to be spared, or hoping—
Or offering more for freedom than the girth
That holds his sword, or, at the most, his dagger ?

RECHA.

That proves for me, my father.   For that reason
He was no actual Templar—only seemed it.

Since never to Jerusalem there came
A captive Templar save to certain death ;
Since none e'er walked Jerusalem so free,
How could one voluntarily, at night,
Have come to save me ?

NATHAN.

Most ingenious, Recha !—
Speak, Daja : 'twas from you I learned he came
A prisoner hither ; you must know yet more.

DAJA.

So runs the story.   It is said, besides,
That Saladin preserved the Templar's life
Because of the resemblance that he bore
A favorite brother.   But as twenty years
Have passed away since this dear brother's death—
His name I know not—know not where he died—
It sounds so—so incredible the whole
May be but fiction.

NATHAN.

Wherefore, Daja, sounds it
Incredible, but that you would believe—
As is the case—things more incredible ?
Why should not Saladin, whose family
Are all so dear to him, in younger days
Have loved one brother with peculiar love ?
Look not two countenances oft alike ?
Are old impressions, therefore, vanished ones ?

Works the same cause no longer one effect?
Since when? Where lies in this the incredible?
I grant you, Daja, it were then for you
No more a miracle. Your miracles
Alone demand—deserve, I mean—belief.

DAJA.

You laugh at me.

NATHAN.

Laughed you not too at me?—
Thus was your rescue still a miracle,
Dear Recha, possible alone to Him
Who oft is pleased to guide, by feeble threads,
The set decrees and purpose absolute
Of kings—his toys, if not his scorn.

RECHA.

.My father,
If I am wrong, not willingly I err.

NATHAN.

Willingly rather learn. See now—a forehead
Arched thus, or so; the outline of a nose
Drawn this way more than that; brows curving so,
Or so, according as the bone is sharp
Or round; a line, crease, angle, spot, a nothing
Upon the face of one wild European—
And you are rescued from the fire in Asia !
Is that no miracle, ye wonder-seekers?
What need to trouble an angel with it then?

2*

DAJA.

What harm—if I may speak—in the belief
An angel rather than a man has saved us?
Feel we not so much nearer brought to Him
Of the deliverance the mysterious cause?

NATHAN.

Pride, Daja, naught but pride! The iron pot
Would have itself be lifted from the fire
By silver tongs, that it may deem itself
A silver pot. Pah! What the harm, you ask?
What harm? What good, I might retort. 'Tis
    nonsense,
Or blasphemy, this "feeling nearer God."
But harm it does—ay, actual harm; for listen:
To your deliverer, be he man or angel,
Would you not both, and you especially,
Desire to render great and various service?
But how perform such service to an angel?
Thank him you can, and sigh to him and pray;
Can melt away in ecstasies before him;
Can keep a fast upon his sacred day;
Can give your charities;—all that is naught.
Your neighbor and yourself are more the gainers,
It seems to me, than he. He grows not fat
By all your fasting; all your charities
Make him not rich; no greater is his glory
For all your ecstasies; his power no greater
For all your faith; is it not so? But man—

DAJA.

A man indeed more opportunity
Had given to serve him.   What our readiness,
God knows.   But he was so above all wants,
Was in and for himself so all-sufficient,
As only angels are or angels can be.

RECHA.

And when at last he vanished—

NATHAN.

                Vanished!   How?
No longer showed himself beneath the palms?
Or have you really further searched for him?

DAJA.

That we have not.

NATHAN.

          Not, Daja?   See what harm!
You cruel enthusiasts!   What if this angel
Had been—been sick?

RECHA.

        Sick!

DAJA.

        Sick!   He cannot be!

RECHA.

A shudder chills me.   Daja, feel—my brow,
So warm but now, is turned to ice!

NATHAN.

A Frank
He is, a stranger to our climate ; young;
To all the hard requirements of his Order—
To hunger, watching, unaccustomed.

RECHA.

Sick !

DAJA.

He only means, that it were possible.

NATHAN.

See, there he lies, without a friend, or gold
To purchase friends—

RECHA.

Alas ! my father !

NATHAN.

Lies
Without attendance, counsel, sympathy—
A prey to sorrows, and perhaps to death.

RECHA.

Where ?   Where ?

NATHAN.

He who for one he never knew
Nor saw—enough it was a human being—
Had leaped into the flames—

DAJA.

Oh, spare her, Nathan !

NATHAN.

Who would not know more nearly, would not see
What he had saved, that he might not be thanked—

DAJA.

Oh, Nathan, spare her—spare her !

NATHAN.
Had no wish
To see again, unless a second time
He might deliver ; for enough for him
It was a human being—

DAJA.
Hush !   Ah, see !

NATHAN.

He, dying, has no other solace, none,
Besides the memory of his deed.

DAJA.
Hush ! hush !
You're killing her.

NATHAN.
And so did you kill him ;
Or so you might have killed him.   Recha ! Recha !
'Tis medicine, not poison, that I give you !
He lives !   Come, be yourself !   He is not sick—
Not even sick !

RECHA.
Quite sure ?   Not dead ?   Not sick ?

NATHAN.

Not surely dead ; for God rewards even here
The good that here is done.   But have you learned
That pious ecstasies are easier far
Than virtuous deeds ; how gladly idleness,
Concealing its true motive from itself,
Would stand excused from virtuous deeds, and plead
Its pious ecstasies instead ?

RECHA.

My father,
Leave, leave your Recha nevermore alone !—
He has but left Jerusalem perhaps ?

NATHAN.

Assuredly.—Yonder a Mussulman,
With curious eye, observes my loaded camels.
Look !   Know you him ?

DAJA.

It is your dervise.

NATHAN.

Who ?

DAJA.

Your dervise ; your antagonist at chess.

NATHAN.

Al-Hafi !   That Al-Hafi !

DAJA.

Treasurer now
Of Saladin.

NATHAN.

Dream you again ?   Al-Hafi !—
'Tis he—'tis he indeed !   He comes toward us.
Quick, back into the house !—What will he tell me ?

SCENE III.

NATHAN *and the* DERVISE.

DERVISE.

Now let your eyes be opened to their widest !

NATHAN.

Is it yourself or not ?   In this attire—
A dervise ?

DERVISE.

Well, why not ?   Can dervises
Be turned to no account whatever then ?

NATHAN.

To plenty.   But I had supposed a dervise,
A genuine dervise, would be turned to none.

. DERVISE.

By the Prophet !   May be I'm no genuine one.
Yet, if one must—

NATHAN.

Must—dervise ?   Dervise must ?
Nay, no man must ; why must a dervise then ?
What must he, pray ?

DERVISE.

What is desired of him
In faith and honor, and he knows is right—
That must a dervise.

NATHAN.

There you speak the truth.
Let me embrace you, man, and call you friend !

DERVISE.

Before you learn to what I've been promoted ?

NATHAN.

In spite of your promotion.

DERVISE.

I'm become
A fellow in the State, perhaps, whose friendship
Were inconvenient.

NATHAN.

I will take the risk,
If but your heart continue dervise still.
The fellow in the State is but your gown.

DERVISE.

But that craves honor too. What think you ? Guess !
What were I at your court ?

NATHAN.

Dervise—no more ;
Unless you might besides be—cook.

DERVISE.

Go to !

I should unlearn my trade with you.   A cook !
Not butler too ?—Confess that Saladin
Could better read me.   I'm his treasurer !

NATHAN.

You—his?

DERVISE.

But of the smaller treasure, mind—
That for his house.   His father holds the greater.

NATHAN.

His house is great.

DERVISE.

Ay, greater than you think ;
For every beggar forms a part of it.

NATHAN.

Yet Saladin is so opposed to beggars—

DERVISE.

He would exterminate them root and branch,
Though he himself thereby be made a beggar.

NATHAN.

I thought so.

DERVISE.

Is one now in fact.   Each day
His treasury contains, at sunset, less
Than nothing.   Let the tide be e'er so high
At morning, long ere noon 'tis all run out.

NATHAN.

Because canals, alike impossible
To fill or stay, are feeding from it.

DERVISE.

Right!

NATHAN.

I know it all.

DERVISE.

When princes are the vultures
Amidst the carrion, that is bad enough;
But when they are the carrion 'midst the vultures,
'Tis ten times worse.

NATHAN.

Oh, never, never that!

DERVISE.

Ah, you may talk!—But come, what will you give
If I resign my office to you?   Eh?

NATHAN.

What yields your office?

DERVISE.

Me indeed not much;
But for yourself 'twould yield abundantly.
For when the tide is low, as low it will be,
Lift up your own flood-gates, advance your money,
And take in interest whatsoe'er you will.

NATHAN.

Perhaps charge interest on the interest
Of interest?

DERVISE.

Yes.

NATHAN.

Till my capital
Becomes all interest.

DERVISE.

That tempts you not?
Then write at once the quittance of our friendship;
For I had counted much on you.

NATHAN.

How so?

DERVISE.

That you would help me hold my post with honor;
Your purse be open always to my need.
You shake your head?

NATHAN.

Let's understand each other.
There's a distinction here.   To you—why not?
Al-Hafi, dervise, shall to all I have
Be ever warmly welcome.   But Al-Hafi, .
The treasurer of the Sultan—he—to him—

DERVISE.

Did I not guess it?—How your goodness ever

Keeps pace with prudence, prudence with your wis-
    dom ;
But patience, and this difference in Al-Hafi,
Shall trouble you no more.—Behold this robe
Of honor that the Sultan decked me with.
Ere it be faded and in rags, fit clothing
For dervise' wear, within Jerusalem
It shall be hanging, while beside the Ganges,
Barefoot and light, I walk the burning sands
Among my teachers.

NATHAN.
Like yourself !

DERVISE.
                And play
At chess with them.

NATHAN.
Your highest good.

DERVISE.
                Consider
What tempted me ;—that I might beg no longer?
Might play the part of rich man amongst beggars?
Might have the power of making in a twinkling
A poor rich man out of the richest beggar?

NATHAN.
Not surely that.

DERVISE.
Far more absurd than that.

The first time in my life I had been flattered,
By Saladin's kind-hearted fancy flattered.

NATHAN.

What fancy?

DERVISE.

That a beggar only knew
The feelings of a beggar ; that a beggar
Alone had learned kind dealings with a beggar.
"Your predecessor," he said, "was cold and harsh.
He gave unkindly, if he gave at all ;
Must always first ungraciously inquire
About the asker—not content to know
He was in want ; he must discover, too,
The reason of the want, and make his gifts,
His stingy gifts, proportionate to that.
Not so Al-Hafi.   So unkindly kind
He will not suffer Saladin to seem.
Al-Hafi is not like those foul, clogged pipes,
That give back troubled and impure the water
That was so clear and still when they received it.
Al-Hafi thinks, Al-Hafi feels with me."
Thus sweetly sang the fowler's voice, and lured
The silly bird within the net.   O fool !
The fool too of a fool !

NATHAN.

But gently, gently,

My dervise !

3*

DERVISE.

What! Is it not foolery
To oppress one's brother-men by hundreds, thou·
    sands—
To waste their strength, to plunder, torture, kill
    them—
Yet wish to appear the savior of a few?
Is it not foolery to try to ape
The mercy of the Highest—who, impartial,
On evil and on good, on field and waste,
Spreadeth Himself abroad in sun and rain—
Yet not to have the overflowing hand
Of the Almighty? Is't not foolery—

NATHAN.

Enough! Have done!

DERVISE.

           Not till I have confessed
My equal foolery. Say, was it none
In me that I was always tracing out
The kindly side of fooleries like these,
As my apology for sharing in them?
Call you that none?

NATHAN.

          Al-Hafi, make all haste
To get into your wilderness again.
I fear lest, living among men, you'll cease
To be a man yourself.

DERVISE.

I fear it too.

Farewell !

NATHAN.

So hasty?   Hold, Al-Hafi, hold !
Fear you the desert will escape?   Stay—stay !
Will he not hear me?   Ho, Al-Hafi—here !
No, he is gone ; and I had asked so gladly
About our Templar : he must know the knight.

———.

SCENE IV.

DAJA *entering hastily.*   NATHAN.

DAJA.

O Nathan, Nathan !

NATHAN.

Well, what is it, Daja ?

DAJA.

He has appeared again—appeared again !

NATHAN.

Who, Daja ?

DAJA.

He !

NATHAN.

He?   When appeared *he* not ?
Aha ! 'tis only *your* he that is *he.*
That is not well ; not though he were an angel.

DAJA.

Beneath the palms he's walking to and fro,
And breaking ever and anon the dates.

NATHAN.

And eating ?   As a Templar ?

DAJA.

                    Tease me not !
Beneath the palm-trees' thickly woven shade
Her greedy eye discovered him, and follows
Unwaveringly ; and she entreats, conjures you,
Without delay, to go to him.   Oh, haste !
She's at her window, and will sign to you
Which way to seek him.   Haste !

NATHAN.

                  · Just from my camels ?
Would that be courteous ?   Haste to him yourself,
And tell him my return.   It was his honor
Alone forbade his entering my house
While I was absent.   He'll be glad to come
When 'tis the father that invites him.   Go,
Say I invite him, cordially invite—

DAJA.

In vain ; he will not come to you.   In short,
He comes not to a Jew.

NATHAN.

                  Yet go ; at least
Detain him—keep at least your eye upon him.
Go first ; I follow instantly.   Go—go !

Scene V.

A square planted with palm-trees, under which the
TEMPLAR *is walking to and fro. A* LAY-BROTHER
*follows him at a little distance, as if he would speak
with him.*

TEMPLAR.

'Tis not from idleness he follows me.
See how he glances towards my hands.—Good
    brother—
Or may I call you father?

LAY-BROTHER.

Brother only.
A poor lay-brother only, at your service.

TEMPLAR.

Good brother, had I aught myself—By heaven,
By heaven, I've nothing—

LAY-BROTHER.

Still, take hearty thanks.
May God return to you a thousand-fold
What you would give me.   For the will it is
That makes the giver—not the gift.   Besides,
I was not sent to beg the knight for alms.

TEMPLAR.

Then you were sent?

LAY-BROTHER.

Yes; from the monastery.

TEMPLAR.

Where I had hoped but now to find a morsel
Of pilgrim's fare?

LAY-BROTHER.

The tables then were filled.
But let the knight return with me.

TEMPLAR.

Why so?
'Tis many a day since I have tasted meat.
Besides, what need?   The dates are ripe.

LAY-BROTHER.

The knight
Should be upon his guard against the fruit;
Too much is dangerous.   It clogs the spleen,
Breeds melancholy.

TEMPLAR.

And if I now prefer
Being melancholy?   But to give that warning
You were not sent.

LAY-BROTHER.

Oh no; I was but sent
To sound the knight somewhat—to feel his pulse.

TEMPLAR.

You tell me that yourself?

LAY-BROTHER.
                    And wherefore not?

TEMPLAR.
(A crafty brother.)   Does the monastery
Have many such as you?

LAY-BROTHER.
                    I do not know.
I must obey, sir knight.

TEMPLAR.
                    So you obey,
And ask no questions?

LAY-BROTHER.
                    Were aught else obeying,
Sir knight?

TEMPLAR.
(See how simplicity is sure
To come off best!)   Could you not further tell
The name of him who seeks such knowledge of me?
My oath, 'tis not yourself.

LAY-BROTHER.
                    Were it becoming
In me, or profitable?

TEMPLAR.
                    Whom could it profit,
Or whom become to be so curious?

LAY-BROTHER.

The Patriarch, I conclude, since he it was
Who sent me here.

TEMPLAR.

      The Patriarch? Knows he not
The white cloak's bloody cross?

LAY-BROTHER.

        Even I know that.

TEMPLAR.

Well then! I am a Templar, and a captive.
And if I add that I was taken at Tebnin,
The fortress that we vainly tried to scale
Before the truce expired, and thus lay open
A passage into Sidon,—if I add,
That twenty more were taken captive with me,
But I alone received the Sultan's pardon,—
Then has the Patriarch all he needs to know—
More than he needs.

LAY-BROTHER.

      Scarce more, though, than he knew,
He fain would know the reason why the knight
Was pardoned by the Sultan—he alone.

TEMPLAR.

I know not that myself. My neck was bared,
And on my mantle kneeling I awaited
The final stroke, when more intent his eyes

The Sultan fixes on me, toward me springs,
And motions. I am raised ; my chains fall off ;
I try to thank him ; tears are in his eyes ;
Silent is he—am I ; he goes, I stay.
What now the meaning of it all may be,
The Patriarch must unriddle for himself.

LAY-BROTHER.

His inference is that God must have reserved you
For great, great enterprises.

TEMPLAR.

         Great indeed !

For rescuing a Jewess from the fire,
Conducting curious pilgrims up Mount Sinai,
And more as great.

LAY-BROTHER.

        The rest will come.   Meanwhile
'Tis not a bad beginning.   Greater things
Already for the knight the Patriarch
May have in store.

TEMPLAR.

        Ah, brother, think you so ?
Has any hint been dropped of such ?

LAY-BROTHER.

            Ay, ay.
But first I am to sound the knight to learn
If he's the man.

TEMPLAR.

All right ; sound on ! (Let's see
How he will sound me !) Well?

LAY-BROTHER.

The shortest way
Were honestly to set before the knight
The Patriarch's wish.

TEMPLAR.

Good !

LAY-BROTHER.

He desires to send
A little letter by the knight.

TEMPLAR.

By me ?
I am no carrier. So then, that's the work
He holds more glorious than the rescuing
A Jewess from the fire ?

LAY-BROTHER.

It must be ; for—
The Patriarch says—upon this little letter
The interests of all Christendom depend.
God will reward the safe delivery of it—
The Patriarch says—with a peculiar crown
In heaven ; and of this crown—the Patriarch says—
Is none more worthy than the knight.

TEMPLAR.

Than I?

LAY-BROTHER.

Because to earn this crown—the Patriarch says—
Is none more fitted than the knight.

TEMPLAR.

Than I?

LAY-BROTHER.

You have your freedom here ; can everything
Examine at your will ; you understand
How cities should be stormed, and how defended ;
Can duly estimate—the Patriarch says—
The strength and weakness of that inner wall
Just built by Saladin ; and can minutely
Describe it to the soldiers of the Cross.

TEMPLAR.

Could you not further tell me the contents,
Good brother, of the letter?

LAY-BROTHER.

     The contents—
I know not quite myself. But to King Philip
The letter is addressed. The Patriarch—
I oft have wondered that a holy man,
Whose walk is else in heaven, should deign to keep
So well informed of the affairs of earth.
It must be very burdensome to him.

TEMPLAR.

Go on; the Patriarch—

LAY-BROTHER.

Knows beyond a doubt
Exactly how and where, with how great force,
From what direction, Saladin will open
The next campaign, should war break out afresh

TEMPLAR.

He does?

LAY-BROTHER.

He does, and would inform King Philip;
That he may judge if danger be so great,
'Twere better to renew at any cost
The truce with Saladin, so lately broken
By your brave Order.

TEMPLAR.

What a Patriarch!
No common messenger he seeks in me,
Good honest man; he wants—a spy. Go, tell him,
As far as you could sound me, worthy brother,
He had mistaken his man; that I am bound
To hold myself still captive; and that Templars
Have one profession, that of arms—know naught
Of playing the spy.

LAY-BROTHER.

I thought so! None the worse
My judgment of the knight. The best remains.

The Patriarch has ferreted out the fortress,
What name it bears, and where on Lebanon
It lies, wherein are stored the enormous sums
From which the Sultan's prudent father pays
The army, and defrays all costs of war.
Thither, from time to time, the Sultan goes,
By lonely roads, and almost unattended.
You understand?

TEMPLAR.

Not I!

LAY-BROTHER.

How easy now
To overpower the Sultan, or—despatch him.
You shudder? Nay; two pious Maronites
Have volunteered already for the deed,
If but some valiant man be found to lead them.

TEMPLAR.

And did the Patriarch look to me again
To be this valiant leader?

LAY-BROTHER.

He believes
That out of Ptolemais can King Philip
Give most effectual aid.

TEMPLAR.

To me—to me?
Have you not heard, have you not just been told,
What obligations bind me to the Sultan?

4*

LAY-BROTHER.

I heard.

TEMPLAR.

And yet—

LAY-BROTHER.

Oh, yes—the Patriarch says—
That may be very well ; but God, your Order—

TEMPLAR.

Change naught ; command no villany !

LAY-BROTHER.

Oh no ;
But then—the Patriarch says—a villany
In man's esteem may not be one in God's.

TEMPLAR.

My life I owe the Sultan. Shall my hand
Rob him of his ?

LAY-BROTHER.

As long—the Patriarch says—
As Saladin remains the enemy
Of Christendom, he can acquire no right
To be your friend.

TEMPLAR.

My friend ? A man to whom
I only would not play the thankless villain.

LAY-BROTHER.

True ; but—the Patriarch says—the debt of thanks

Is cancelled, cancelled before God and man,
For service rendered on account of others.
And as—the Patriarch says—it is reported
The Sultan spared you only for a something,
In face or bearing, that recalled a brother—

TEMPLAR.

That too the Patriarch knew; and even yet—
Oh were I sure of that! Ah, Saladin!
Could Nature fashion but a single feature
In likeness of your brother, yet my soul
Receive no answering trait; or could such trait,
To do a Patriarch's pleasure, be suppressed?
Nature, so liest thou not; not so does God
Belie himself upon his works! Go, brother;
Provoke me not to anger. Go!

LAY-BROTHER.

           I go;
And readier than I came. Forgive me, knight.
We brothers have no choice but to obey.

SCENE VI.

The TEMPLAR *and* DAJA. DAJA *has been watching
from a distance, and now approaches.*

DAJA.

The brother's visit left him not, methinks,
In happiest humor. Still, I needs must venture.

TEMPLAR.

Ah, excellent! The proverb holds—the monk
And woman, woman and monk, are Satan's claws.
To-day he throws me to and fro between them.

DAJA.

Do I again behold you, noble knight?
Thank God a thousand times! But where so long
Have you been hiding? Not been sick, I hope?

TEMPLAR.

No.

DAJA.

Well, then?

TEMPLAR

Yes.

DAJA.

We have been anxious for you.

TEMPLAR.

Indeed!

DAJA.

Have you been on a journey?

TEMPLAR.

Yes.

DAJA.

And just returned to-day?

TEMPLAR.

No; yesterday.

DAJA.

To-day has Recha's father too returned.
Now may not Recha hope?

TEMPLAR.

For what?

DAJA.

For that
She has so often begged.   Her father too
Will soon himself most pressingly invite you.
He comes from Babylon, with twenty camels
Piled high with precious spices, stones, and stuffs,
The rich returns of India, Persia, Syria—
Of China even.

TEMPLAR

I do not buy.

DAJA.

His people
Revere him as a prince ; yet why 'the wise'
They call him, not 'the rich,' I often wonder.

TEMPLAR.

To them, perchance, are rich and wise the same.

DAJA.

Good should they call him first.   How good he is
You cannot think.   When Recha's debt to you
Was told him, there was nothing in that moment
He'd not have done for you or given.

TEMPLAR.
                                   Indeed !
DAJA.
Try him, and see !

TEMPLAR.
              How soon a moment passes ?

DAJA.
Were he less good, should I have been content
So long to dwell with him ?   You think, perhaps,
I do not feel my dignity as Christian ?
No song beside my baby-cradle told
That only for this cause to Palestine
I should accompany my wedded lord,
There to bring up a Jewish girl.   My husband,
A noble squire in Emperor Frederick's army—

TEMPLAR.
By birth a Swiss, to whom had been accorded
The glory of drowning in the selfsame stream
With his Imperial Majesty.   O woman,
How often have you told me that before ?
Is there no end to your pursuing me ?

DAJA.
Pursuing ?

TEMPLAR.
              Yes, pursuing.   I'll not see
Nor hear you more ; I will not be reminded
Forever by you of a deed I did

Without a thought ; a riddle to myself
Whene'er I think of it. Not willingly
Would I repent it ; but should such a chance
Again occur, you'll have yourself to blame
If I'm a trifle slower, stop to question,
And let what's burning, burn.

DAJA.

May God forbid !

TEMPLAR.

From this day forth, grant me at least the favor
Of knowing me no more. I beg it of you.
Keep too the father from me. Jew is Jew.
I am a clumsy Swabian. Long ago
The maiden's image faded from my soul,
If it were ever there.

DAJA.

Not yours from hers.

TEMPLAR.

And what of that ?

DAJA.

Who knows ?   Men are not always)
The thing they seem.

TEMPLAR.

Yet seldom better.   [*Is going.*

DAJA.

Stay ;

Why haste you ?

TEMPLAR.

Woman, do not make these palms,
'Neath which I've loved to walk, grow hateful to me.

DAJA.

Go then, you Northern bear! Go—go! And yet
I must not lose the monster out of sight.

[*She follows him at a distance.*]

ACT SECOND.

Scene I.

Room in the Sultan's palace. Saladin *and* Sittah
at chess.

Sittah.
Where are you, Saladin? Why, how you play!

Saladin.
Not well? I thought I did.

Sittah.
For me : yet hardly.
Take back that move.

Saladin.
Why so?

Sittah.
The knight's exposed.

Saladin.
True : so, then !

Sittah.
Then shall I step in between.

Saladin.
You're right again. Then check !

5

SITTAH.

What use in that?
I interpose, and you are where you were.

SALADIN.

From this dilemma is there no escape,
Except by paying.   Well, then take my knight.

SITTAH.

I want him not; I let him stand.

SALADIN.

No favor.
The place was more important than the piece.

SITTAH.

May be.

SALADIN.

But reckon not without your host.
See! had you looked for that?

SITTAH.

I'd not, indeed;
How could I think you weary of your queen?

SALADIN.

My queen?

SITTAH.

Beyond my thousand denarii,
No fraction shall I win to-day, I see.

SALADIN.

How so?

SITTAH.

You ask?   Because with all your might
You will be beaten.   That's no gain to me.
Small pleasure can one take in games like that.
Besides, win I not always most from you
When I have lost?   When have you failed to send
The double of the stake, to comfort me
For my defeat?

SALADIN.

Ah! so, my little sister,
When you have lost, you lost on purpose—eh?

SITTAH.

Your generosity at least, dear brother,
May be to blame that I'm no better player.

SALADIN.

But we forget our game.   Come, make an end!

SITTAH.

How stands it?   So then, check, and double check!

SALADIN.

That double check I truly had not seen.
It robs me of my queen.

SITTAH.

Could you have helped it?
Let's see!

SALADIN.

No, no; take off the queen.   I ne'er
Was lucky with the piece.

SITTAH.

Only the piece?

SALADIN.

Away with her!   No harm is done; for thus
All's safe again.

SITTAH.

Well has my brother taught
The courtesy that should be showed to queens.

                                        [*Leaves her.*

SALADIN.

Take her or take her not!   I have no other.

SITTAH.

Why should I take her?   Check! check!

SALADIN.

                              Keep on!

SITTAH.

                                        Check!
And check! and check!

SALADIN.

                    And mate!   .

SITTAH.

                    Not quite; your knight
Can interpose, or what you will; all one.

SALADIN.

Right!   You have won, and Hafi pays.   Go, call
him!—

You guessed aright, dear Sittah ; for my mind
Was not intent upon the game—it wandered.
Besides, who gives us these smooth pieces always,
That have no meaning, no suggestion in them ?
Have I then played with the Imam himself ?—
Defeat but seeks excuse.   'Twas not alone
The shapeless pieces, Sittah, made me lose.
Your skill, your sharper, quicker eye—

SITTAH.

There too
You would but blunt the sting of your defeat.
Enough, you were preoccupied ; even more
Than I.

SALADIN.

Than you ?   What had you on your mind ?

SITTAH.

Not your anxiety.—O Saladin,
When shall we play so heartily again ?

SALADIN.

We'll play but so much the more greedily.
Because there's to be war again, you mean ?
So be it !   On !   Not I the first to draw.
I gladly would have had the truce renewed ;
Gladly, most gladly, would have given my Sittah
A noble husband, too, as Richard's brother
Had surely been.   Is he not Richard's brother ?

SITTAH.

Ah, if you can but sing your Richard's praises !

5*

SALADIN.

If Richard's sister, then, could have become
Our brother Melech's wife— Ah, what a house !
Of all the best, first houses in the world,
The best, the first.   You see I am not slow
To praise myself.   I do not deem myself
Unworthy of my friends.   What men had then
Been born into the world !

SITTAH.

Did I not laugh
From the beginning at your beauteous dreams?
You do not know, you will not know the Christians,
· Christianity, not manhood, is their pride.
E'en that which from their founder down has spiced
Their superstition with humanity,
'Tis not for its humanity they love it.
No ; but because Christ taught, Christ practised it.
Happy for them he was so good a man !
Happy for them that they can trust his virtue !
His virtue?   Not his virtue, but his name,
They say, shall spread abroad, and shall devour
And put to shame the names of all good men.
The name, the name is all their pride.

SALADIN.

Why else,
You think, should they require of you and Melech
To take the Christian name, ere you could love
A Christian consort?

SITTAH.

Yes ; as if in Christians,
As Christians only, could exist that love
With which, in the beginning, God endowed
Both man and woman.

SALADIN.

Poor conceits too many
The Christians hold, not to believe that also.
And yet you err.   The Templars, not the Christians,
Are here to blame ; are not to blame as Christians,
But Templars.   They it is who bring our plans
To naught.   They will not lose their hold on Acca,
Which Richard's sister, as her dower, would bring
To Melech.   Lest the knightly interest
Should suffer loss, they play the silly monk.
A sudden blow they think may have success,
And scarce can wait until the truce be o'er.—
Keep on, my masters, on !   I'm well content.
Were but all else as I would have it !

SITTAH.

What ?
What else disturbed you—so could ruffle you ?

SALADIN.

What always has disturbed me.   I have been
Upon Mount Lebanon ; I've seen our father.
His cares still burden him.

SITTAH.

Alas !

SALADIN.
                          Escape
There's none ; on every side he's cramped; feels
     lack,
Now here, now there.

SITTAH.
          What is it lacks ?   What cramps him ?

SALADIN.
What else but that I hardly deign to name ;
Which, when I have, seems worthless ; but when not,
Is indispensable ?—Where tarries Hafi ?
Was he not called ?—This fatal, cursed gold !
Good, Hafi, that you're come.

SCENE II.

The dervise AL-HAFI.   SALADIN.   SITTAH.

AL-HAFI.
               The gold from Egypt
Has then arrived.   There need be plenty of it.

SALADIN.
Have you had tidings ?

AL-HAFI.
          I ?   Not I !   I came
Expecting to receive them.

SALADIN.
Pay to Sittah
A thousand denarii.

[*Walks to and fro, lost in thought.*

AL-HAFI.
Pay—not receive !
That's good ! A something rather less than naught.
To Sittah ? Once again to Sittah ? Lost ?
And lost again at chess ! There stands the game.

SITTAH.
You cannot grudge me my good fortune ?

AL-HAFI (*studying the game*).
Grudge ?
If— But you know.

SITTAH (*motioning to him*).
Hush, Hafi, hush !

AL-HAFI (*still looking on the board*).
'Twere better
You grudged yourself.

SITTAH.
Hush, Hafi !

AL-HAFI (*to Sittah*).
Yours the white ?
You offer check ?

SITTAH.
'Tis well he does not hear.

AL-HAFI.

The move is his?

SITTAH (*going nearer to him*).

Pray, say I may receive
My money.

AL-HAFI (*still intent on the game*).

Yes; you shall receive the money,
As you receive it always.

SITTAH.

Are you mad?

AL-HAFI.

The game's not over, Saladin—not lost.

SALADIN (*scarce attending*).

No matter! Pay!

AL-HAFI.

Pay—pay!—There stands your queen.

SALADIN.

She counts for naught; belongs not in the game.

SITTAH.

Make haste and say that I may fetch the money.

AL-HAFI (*still eager with the game*).

Of course; as usual.—But suppose the queen
Be no more in the game, you're not yet mated.

SALADIN (*approaches and overturns the board*).
I am ; I will be.

AL-HAFI.
So ! As played, so won !
And as 'twas won, so 'twill be paid.

SALADIN (*to Sittah*).
What says he ?

SITTAH (*occasionally signing to Al-Hafi*).
You know him ; know he likes to make objections,
And to be urged ; is e'en a trifle jealous.

SALADIN.
But not of you ? Not of my sister ?—Hafi,
What hear I of you ? Jealous ?

AL-HAFI.
May be so.
I would I had her mind ; were good as she.

SITTAH.
Still, he has always paid me honestly ;
To-day, too, will he pay. Trust him.—Go, Hafi !
I'll send and fetch the money.

AL-HAFI.
No ; I play
This farce with you no more. He must be told.

SALADIN.
Who ? What ?

SITTAH.

Al-Hafi, keep you thus your word?
Is this your promise?

AL-HAFI.

How could I suppose
You'd carry it so far?

SALADIN.

Shall I learn naught?

SITTAH.

I pray you, Hafi, be discreet.

SALADIN.

'Tis strange!
Does Sittah pray so earnestly, so warmly
A stranger's and a dervise's forbearance,
Rather than mine, her brother's?   I command,
Al-Hafi!   Dervise, speak!

SITTAH.

Let not a trifle
Disturb you, brother, more than it deserves.
You know that many times I've won from you
This same amount at chess; and since the money
To me was useless now, and Hafi's chest
Had none too much of it, I left it there.
But have no fear, for neither you, my brother,
Nor Hafi, nor the treasury, shall keep it.

AL-HAFI.

Ah, if that were but all!

SITTAH.

With more such trifles.
The allowance once you granted me, that too
Has in the treasury been left : some months
It has been left undrawn.

AL-HAFI.

E'en that's not all.

SALADIN.

Not all ?   Speak out, then !

AL-HAFI.

Since we've been expecting
The gold from Egypt, she—

SITTAH (*to Saladin*).

Why listen to him ?

AL-HAFI.

Not only drew no money, but—

SALADIN.

Advanced
Her own ?—not so !

AL-HAFI.

Supported the whole court.
Herself alone defrayed your whole expense.

SALADIN (*embracing her*).

My own true sister !

6

SITTAH.

Who but you, my brother,
Had made me rich enough to do so much?

AL-HAFI.

And now is making her as poor, as beggared
As he himself.

SALADIN.

I poor?   Her brother poor?
When had I more—when less?   A cloak, a sword,
A horse—and God !   What need I more ?   In these,
When can I want?   Yet could I chide you, Hafi.

SITTAH.

Nay, chide not, brother.   Could I but relieve
Our father's needs as well !

SALADIN.

Ah, there you dash
My happiness again.   I, for myself,
Want nothing—cannot want.   But he—he wants;
And in him, want we all.   What shall I do?
It may be long before the gold arrives
From Egypt.   Why so great delay, God knows.
All's quiet there.   I will economize,
Will save, submit to aught that but concerns
Myself, and brings no suffering on others.
But what avails it all?   A horse, a cloak,
A sword—these must I have ; and with my God
There is no cheapening. · Little enough it is

Contents him now—my heart.   I counted much
Upon your treasury's overplus, Al-Hafi.

AL-HAFI.

My overplus?   Confess yourself, empaling,
Or strangling at the least, had been my doom,
If any overplus you'd caught me in.
A fraud, indeed, had been a safer venture.

SALADIN.

What's to be done?—Was there, then, none but
    Sittah
To borrow of?

SITTAH.

    Would I that privilege,
My brother, have relinquished?   Still I claim it.
Still not quite to the bottom am I drained.

SALADIN.

Not quite!   That's worst of all.—Take instant
    measures ;
Get gold of whom you can, and as you can ;
Go, borrow—promise !   Only borrow not
Of those made rich by me ; such borrowing
Were asking back my gifts.   Seek the most greedy:
They readiest lend to me ; for they have learned
How in my hands their gold accumulates.

AL-HAFI.

I know none such.

SITTAH.

I just bethink me, Hafi,
I heard your friend was back again.

AL-HAFI (*embarrassed*).

My friend?
Who may he be?

SITTAH.

That much-praised Jew of yours.

AL-HAFI.

A much-praised Jew—of mine?

SITTAH.

Endowed by God,—
I well remember yet the words you used
In speaking of him,—one endowed by God
In fullest measure with the least and greatest
Of all this world's possessions.

AL-HAFI.

Said I so?
What could such words have meant?

SITTAH.

The least is riches;
The greatest, wisdom.

AL-HAFI.

Of a Jew?   What Jew
Could words like those have fitted?

SITTAH.

Not your Nathan?

AL-HAFI.

Ah, Nathan—yes; I had not thought of him.
Is he indeed come back again at last?
Things must have prospered with him then. 'Tis
true,
The people called him once the Wise—and Rich.

SITTAH.

Now more than ever call they him the Rich.
The city rings with stories of the jewels,
The treasures he has brought.

AL-HAFI.

So then the Rich
He is again, and soon will be the Wise.

SITTAH.

What say you to approaching him, Al-Hafi?

AL-HAFI.

For what? You do not mean to borrow? Ah,
There you mistake him. Nathan lend! Therein
Consists his wisdom, that he lends to none.

SITTAH.

Another picture of him once you drew.

AL-HAFI.

He'd lend you merchandise at need; but money,
His money, never! Otherwise a Jew,

6*

Whose like is rarely found among his people.
He has intelligence, knows how to live,
Is strong at chess.   But he excels the rest
In evil as in good.   Count not on him.
'Tis true, he gives the poor.   A match he is
For Saladin, in giving.   Not as much,
Perhaps, but just as gladly—just as free
From all distinction.   Mussulman, Parsee,
The Christian, or the Jew, all one to him.

SITTAH.

And such a man—

SALADIN.

How can I ne'er have heard
Of such a man till now !

SITTAH.

Would he not lend
To Saladin—to Saladin, who spends
For others only, not himself?

AL-HAFI.

There shows
The Jew again—the ordinary Jew.
My word for it, so envious he is,
So jealous of your giving !   No " God bless you !"
In all the world, but he'd have said to him.
He therefore lends to none, lest he should lose
The means of giving.   Charity his law
Commands, but it commands not courtesy ;
And thus through charity is he become

The most discourteous neighbor in the world.
'Tis true, we've not been on good terms of late ;
But think me not for that unjust to him.
In all else is he good, but not to lend :
Trust me he's not.—I'll knock at other doors.
I just bethink me of a Moor who's rich
And miserly.—I go ! I go !

SITTAH.

What haste,

Al-Hafi?

SALADIN.

Let him go : nay, let him go !

SCENE III.

SITTAH. SALADIN.

SITTAH.

He hurries off as he were glad to escape.
What means it ?   Has he been himself deceived,
Or would he mislead us?

SALADIN.

Why ask of me?

I hardly know of whom you spoke.   This Nathan,
This Jew of yours, I never heard his name
Until to-day.

SITTAH.

How is it possible
You never heard of one of whom 'tis said
He has explored the graves of Solomon
And David, and by certain magic words
Can loose their seals?   And further, that from them
He brings to light of day, from time to time,
That boundless wealth which speaks no lesser source.

SALADIN.

If 'tis from graves this man derives his wealth,
'Tis surely not from Solomon's or David's,
But from the graves of fools !

SITTAH.

                    Or knaves !   Besides,
More yielding are the sources of his wealth
Than such a mammon-pit ; exhaustless are they.

SALADIN.

He trades, you say.

SITTAH.

                    His beasts of burden toil
On every highway and through every desert ;
In every harbor lie his ships.   Al-Hafi
So told me once, and rapturously added
How generously, nobly would his friend
Employ the wealth he had not thought too mean
To labor for with hand and brain : he added,
How free from prejudice his spirit was,

How open was his heart to every virtue,
With all things beautiful in sympathy.

SALADIN.

Yet now Al-Hafi spoke so doubtfully,
So coldly of him!

SITTAH.

Coldly ?—no ; embarrassed.
As deemed he it were dangerous to praise,
Yet would not censure undeservedly.
Or is it that the best among his people
Can never quite escape the Jew ; that here
Is Hafi disappointed in his friend ?
But be he what he may—more than a Jew
Or less—is he but rich, enough for us.

SALADIN.

You surely would not take his gold from him
By violence, dear sister !

SITTAH.

Violence ?
What call you violence ? by fire and sword ?
No, no ; against the weak what force is needed
Save their own weakness ?—Come with me awhile
Into my harem ; you must hear a singer
I bought me yesterday.   I've a design
On Nathan shall meanwhile be ripening.   Come !

Scene IV.

Near the palms before Nathan's *house.* Recha *and*
Nathan *come from the house.* Daja *joins them.*

Recha.

Why have you been so long in coming, father?
You scarce will find him now.

Nathan.

        Well, well; if here
No more, no longer 'neath these palms, yet else-
  where.
Be tranquil. See, comes there not Daja to us?

Recha.

She's lost him, I am sure.

Nathan.

     Perhaps not, Recha.

Recha.

She'd come more quickly else.

Nathan.

      She may not see us. . . .

Recha.

She sees us now.

Nathan.

    And hurries forward. Look!
Be calm—be quiet!

RECHA.

Would you want a child
Who could be calm,—who could be unconcerned
For one whose bravery was her life—the life
She values only as it came from you?

NATHAN.

I would not have you other than you are ;
Not though I read a something in your soul
You will not name.

RECHA.
What, father?

NATHAN.

Do you ask—
Ask me so timidly? Whate'er be stirred
Within you, 'tis but innocence and nature.
Fear not. I have no fear. But promise me—
If e'er your heart declare itself more plainly,
No wish of it shall be concealed from me.

RECHA.

You make me tremble but to think my heart
Could ever wish concealment from my father.

NATHAN.

Enough ; 'tis once for all agreed between us.—
See, here is Daja !—Well?

DAJA.

He's walking yet
Beneath the palms, just hid by yonder wall.
Look, there he is !

RECHA.

Ah, see !   He hesitates.
Will he go on or back, to right or left?

DAJA.

No, no ; he's sure to take again the path
Around the cloister, and must pass this way.

RECHA.

Right, right !   Say, have you spoken with him to-
day?
How is he?

DAJA.

Just as always.

NATHAN.

Have a care
He does not see you.   Better further back ;—
Or safest in the house.

RECHA.

But one look more !
Alas, the hedge that steals him from me !

DAJA.

Come !
Your father's right.   He might turn back at once,
Should he behold you.   Come !

RECHA.

Ah me, that hedge !

NATHAN.

And should he suddenly emerge from it,
He could not fail to see you. Go, then—go !

DAJA.

Come, come with me ; I'll take you to a window,
Whence we may watch them unobserved. Come !

· RECHA.

Yes ?
[*Both into the house.*

———

SCENE V.

NATHAN. *Soon afterward the* TEMPLAR.

NATHAN.

I almost dread to meet this strange Unknown ;
I almost shrink before his rugged virtue.
Strange that one man can make his fellow-man
Thus ill at ease !—Ah, there he comes. By heaven !
A manly youth. That brave, defiant look,
I like it well—that solid tread. The shell
Alone is bitter ; surely not the kernel.
Where have I seen one like him ?—Noble **Frank,**
Forgive me—

TEMPLAR.

What?

NATHAN.

Permit me—

TEMPLAR.
                    What, Jew, what?
NATHAN.
That I presume to address you.

TEMPLAR.
                         Can I help it?
Be brief!

NATHAN.
         Forgive, and hurry not so proudly,
With such contempt, past one whom you have bound
Unto yourself forever.

TEMPLAR.
                   How is that?
Ah, I can guess.   You are—

NATHAN.
                    My name is Nathan;
I'm father of the maiden whom you saved
So generously from the fire.   I come—

TEMPLAR.
If 'tis to thank me, you may spare yourself.
Too many thanks have I endured already
For such a trifle.   Nothing do you owe me.
How did I know the maiden was your daughter?
It is the Templar's duty to assist
The first, the best whose need he sees.   Besides,
My life was at that moment hateful to me.
I gladly seized the opportunity

To risk it for another—for another,
Though but a Jewess.

NATHAN.

It is nobly spoken—
Offensively and nobly. Yet I read
Your motive. Modest greatness shields itself
Behind offensive words from admiration.
But if it scorn the tribute of our praise,
Is there none other less contemptible?
Knight, were you not a prisoner here, a stranger,
I should not be thus bold. Command me—speak!
What service can be done you?

TEMPLAR.

None by you.

NATHAN.

Yet I am rich.

TEMPLAR.

To me the richest Jew
Was ne'er the best.

NATHAN.

Might you not still employ
That better which he has—employ his wealth?

TEMPLAR.

Good; there I will not wholly say you nay—
E'en for my mantle's sake. When this be worn
To tatters, so that neither shred nor stitch
Will hold together longer, I will come

And borrow cloth or money for a new one.—
Look not so troubled.   You are safe a while.
'Tis not yet come to that.   See, it is still
In tolerable condition.   Only here
It has an ugly spot ; this end was scorched.
But lately did it happen, as I bore
Your daughter through the fire.

NATHAN (*taking hold of the corner and looking at it*).
                    Strange that a burn,
An ugly spot like that, should bear this man
A better testimony than his lips !—
Might I but kiss it—kiss the spot !   Ah, pardon,
'Twas unawares.

                    TEMPLAR.
            What ?

                    NATHAN.
                That a tear fell on it.

                    TEMPLAR.
No matter, it has had such drops before.
(I soon shall grow confused before this Jew.)

                    NATHAN.
Might I request the further favor of you,
That you would send your mantle to my daughter ?

                    TEMPLAR.
What would she with it ?

NATHAN.

That her lips may press
The spot, since to embrace your knees, in vain
Is her desire.

TEMPLAR.

But, Jew—your name is Nathan?
But, Nathan—you have spoken well, and sharply.
I know not what to answer.   Surely—I—

NATHAN.

Disguise yourself, dissemble as you will.
Here too I've found you out.   You were too good,
Too honorable to be more polite.
A girl, all sentiment—her waiting woman,
All eagerness to serve—her father absent—
You cared for her good name ; fled from her gaze—
Fled that you might not conquer.   Further cause
For thanks.

TEMPLAR.

I must confess you know the motives
That ought to be a Templar's.

NATHAN.

But a Templar's?
Ought only—and because his Order bids?
I know a good man's motives, and I know
Good men are everywhere.

TEMPLAR.

With no distinction?

NATHAN.

Distinguished by their color, form, and dress.

TEMPLAR.

Not more or less in one place than another?

NATHAN.

All such distinctions are of small account.
The great man everywhere needs ample space :
Too many, closely planted, dash themselves
Against each other.   Average ones, like us,
Stand everywhere in crowds.   But let not one
Cast slurs upon the others.   Knots and gnarls
Must live on friendly terms.   One little peak
Must not take airs, as 'twere the only one
Not sprung from earth.

TEMPLAR.

              Well said !   But know you, Nathan,
What people practised first this casting slurs—
What people were the first to call themselves
The chosen people?   How if I—not hate,
Indeed—but cannot help despising them
For all their pride,—a pride which has descended
To Mussulman and Christian,—that their God
Must be the one true God?   You start to hear
Such words from me, a Christian and a Templar.
When, where, has this fanaticism of having
The better God, and forcing him as best
On all the world, e'er showed itself in colors

More black than here and now? Who here and now
Feels not his eyes unsealed—But be he blind
Who will!—Forget what I have said, and leave me.
[*Going.*

NATHAN.

You know not how much closer you have drawn me.
We must, we must be friends! Despise my people
With all your heart. We neither chose our people.
Are we our people? What does "people" mean?
Is Jew or Christian rather Jew or Christian
Than man? May I have found in you another
Who is content to be esteemed a man!

TEMPLAR.

You have, by heaven, you have! Your hand! I blush
That for a moment I should have misjudged you.

NATHAN.

And I am proud; for 'tis the vulgar only
That rarely is misjudged.

TEMPLAR.

And but the rare
That's not forgotten. Nathan, yes, we must,
We must indeed be friends.

NATHAN.

Are so already.
How Recha will rejoice! And ah, how bright
The future opens to me! Only know her!

TEMPLAR.

I'm burning with impatience.   Who is this
Comes running from your house—is it not Daja?

NATHAN.

'Tis she—but why so troubled?

TEMPLAR.

                    Oh, may naught
Have happened to our Recha !

———

SCENE VI.

The preceding.   DAJA *enters hastily.*

DAJA.

                    Nathan, Nathan !

NATHAN.

Well?

DAJA.

Pardon me that I disturb you, knight.

NATHAN.

What is it?

TEMPLAR.

        What?

DAJA.

The Sultan sends.
The Sultan wants to see you. Oh, good heaven !
The Sultan !

NATHAN.

Me ?—the Sultan ?   He desires
To see what novelties I've brought ; but tell him
That little—nothing has been yet unpacked.

DAJA.

Naught will he see ; he wants to speak with you,
With you in person, soon, as soon as may be.

NATHAN.

I come.   Go, go !

DAJA.

Be not displeased, dread knight.
We're so concerned to know the Sultan's pleasure !

NATHAN.

That will be known in time.   Go, leave us now !

———

SCENE VII.

NATHAN *and the* TEMPLAR.

TEMPLAR.

Then know you him not personally yet ?

NATHAN.

The Sultan ?   No.   I've neither shunned nor sought
    him.
The common fame spoke far too well of him
For me not rather to believe than see.
But now—though that be false, his saving of your
    life—

TEMPLAR.

Yes ; that at least is true.   I hold my life
But as his gift.

NATHAN.

                He granted me with that
A double, threefold life.   That changes all
Between us ; throws a sudden net about me
Which binds me to his service evermore.
Scarce can I wait to learn his first commands.
I am prepared for all ; and will confess
I am so for your sake.

TEMPLAR.

                Oft as I've met him
I've found no way to thank him yet myself.
The impression that I made upon him came
As suddenly as suddenly it passed.
It may be he remembers me no more :
Yet once at least he must remember me,
To speak my final sentence.   Not enough
That I exist at his command ; have life

But by his will : he must decide whose will
Shall guide my life.

NATHAN.

True : I will haste the more.
Some word may furnish opportunity
To speak of you.   Permit me—pardon— I haste.
When will you come to us?

TEMPLAR.

Whene'er I may.

NATHAN.

Whene'er you will.

TEMPLAR.

To-day, then.

NATHAN.

And your name,
I pray you?

TEMPLAR.

Was—is Curd von Stauffen.   Curd !

NATHAN.

Von Stauffen—Stauffen?

TEMPLAR.

Does the name surprise you?

NATHAN.

Von Stauffen ?   Many of that name have here—

TEMPLAR.

Oh yes ; full many here have lived and died.
My uncle—father— But why fix your eyes
With such a growing eagerness upon me?

NATHAN.

Oh, nothing, nothing ! Can I e'er be weary
Of gazing on you ?

TEMPLAR.

Then I leave you first.
The seeker's eye not seldom has discovered
More than the seeker wished. I dread it, Nathan.
Let time, not curiosity, cement
Our friendship. [*He goes.*

NATHAN.

Oft the seeker's eye discovers
More than he wished.—He seemed to read my soul
That might befall me here.—'Tis not alone
Wolf's gait, Wolf's figure, but his voice as well.
Exactly so would Wolf throw back his head ;
So carried Wolf his sword ; so Wolf would shade
His brow to hide the flashing of his eyes.
How such deep-printed images will slumber
Within us, till a word, a sound awakes them !
Von Stauffen—that was it. Filneck and Stauffen.
Of this I must know more, and presently.
But first to Saladin.—Who's listening there?
Is it not Daja ? Come, come nearer, Daja.

Scene VIII.

Daja. Nathan.

Nathan.

What is it? Ah, the weight on both your hearts
Is not what Saladin would have with me.

Daja.

You cannot blame her for it. At the moment
Your converse with him grew more intimate,
The Sultan's message drove us from the window.

Nathan.

Tell her she may expect him every moment.

Daja.

In truth?

Nathan.

May I depend upon you, Daja?
Be on your guard, I pray you. You will ne'er
Have reason to repent it. E'en your conscience
Will find account in it. Disturb me not
In what I plan. In all you ask and tell,
Use caution and reserve.

Daja.

That you should think
I needed to be warned! I go : go you!
For see, there surely comes from Saladin
A second messenger—your dervise, Hafi. [*Goes.*
8

Scene IX.

Nathan. Al-Hafi.

Al-Hafi.

Ha, ha !   I'm just in search of you again.

Nathan.

Is it so urgent?   What's his will with me?

Al-Hafi.

Whose?

Nathan.

Saladin's.—I come ; I come.

Al-Hafi.

                   To whom ?

To Saladin ?

Nathan.

Did Saladin not send you ?

Al-Hafi.

No.   Has he sent before?

Nathan.

                He has indeed.

Al-Hafi.

It is decided then.

Nathan.

        What?   What's decided ?

Al-Hafi.

That— I am not to blame ; God knows I'm not.
What tales have I not told of you, what lies,
To avert it ?

Nathan.

What to avert ?   What is decided ?

Al-Hafi.

That you're his treasurer.   I pity you.
At least I'll not stay by to see.   I go ;
I go this hour.   You know already whither,
And know the way.   Have you commands for me
Upon the road ?   Speak ! I am at your service.
But order nothing more than can be carried
Upon a naked back.   Speak quick !   I'm off !

Nathan.

Bethink yourself, Al-Hafi ; pray, consider
That I know nothing yet.   What means your talk ?

Al-Hafi.

Best take the bags with you at once.

Nathan.

           The bags ?

Al-Hafi.

The gold you're to advance to Saladin.

Nathan.

So that is all ?

AL-HAFI.
Shall I look on and see
How he will drain your marrow day by day,
Down to the very toes ; look on and see
How his extravagance will borrow, borrow,
And borrow from those barns ne'er emptied yet
By your wise charities, till the poor mouse
That had its birth there shall be starved to death?
Do you imagine he who needs your gold
Will take your counsel also?   He take counsel!
Took Saladin e'er counsel?   Hear what happened
When last I went to him.

NATHAN.
Well?

AL-HAFI.
I arrived
When Sittah and himself had been at chess.
His sister plays not badly.   There the game
That Saladin had given up for lost
Was standing on the board.   I glanced at it,
And saw that it was far from lost.

NATHAN.
Aha!
A great discovery for you.

AL-HAFI.
His king
But needed to advance upon the pawn
Against her check.   If I could only show you!

NATHAN.

I'll take your word for it.

AL-HAFI

For so the rook
Were brought into the field, and she were lost.
All that I wished to show, and called him.—Think!

NATHAN.

He was not of your mind?

AL-HAFI.

He would not listen;
Contemptuously overturned the board.

NATHAN.

Is't possible?

AL-HAFI.

And said he would be mated.
He would be mated!   Do you call that playing?

NATHAN.

Hardly indeed; 'tis playing with the game.

AL-HAFI.

And that for no mean stake.

NATHAN.

Gold here, gold there!
That is the least.   But not to listen to you

8*

Upon a point so weighty—not to listen,
And not admire your eagle eye—that, that
Cries out for vengeance—does it not?

AL-HAFI.

Nay, nay;
I do but tell you this to show the man.
I'm at the end of all my patience with him.
Here must I run about 'mongst dirty Moors,
And ask who'll lend him.   I who for myself
Have never begged, must borrow now for others.
To borrow scarce is better than to beg;
As lending, lending upon interest,
Scarce better is than stealing.   With my Ghebers
Beside the Ganges have I need of neither,
And need not to become the tool of either.
Beside the Ganges only are there men.
Here none but you is worthy of the life
Beside the Ganges.   Will you come with me?
Leave all your trumpery at once for him,
That he's so anxious for.   By small degrees
He'd have it out of you.   Thus would the torment
At once be ended.   I will get your delk.*
Come, come!

NATHAN.

That deemed I always open to us.
Yet I'll consider it, Al-Hafi.   Wait—

---

* The garb of a dervise.

AL-HAFI.

Consider it! No, no; 'tis not a matter
To be considered.

NATHAN.

Only till I've seen
The Sultan—only till I've said farewell—

AL-HAFI.

He who considers does but seek excuse
For lack of courage. Who cannot resolve
Upon the instant for himself to live,
Remains forevermore the slave of others.
Do as you will!—Farewell!—As you think best!
Here lies my road, there yours.

NATHAN.

Al-Hafi, stay!
You'll settle your affairs before you go?

AL-HAFI.

Oh, pshaw! The treasury holds nought worth count-
ing.
And for my own affairs—why, you or Sittah
Must be my bail. Farewell!   [*Goes.*

NATHAN.

I'll be your bail.
Wild, noble, good—how shall I call him? Truly,
The genuine beggar is the only king.

ACT THIRD.

SCENE I.

Room in Nathan's house. RECHA. DAJA.

RECHA.

Tell me my father's words again, dear Daja.
Said he I might expect him every moment.
Does it not sound as if he'd soon be here?
And yet how many moments have gone by
Since then! Ah well, who thinks of them, the past?
I'll only live in every coming moment.
The one that brings him must be here at last.

DAJA.

Oh that unlucky message from the Sultan!
Else Nathan would have brought him in that instant.

RECHA.

And were it here—that moment; were the warmest,
The fondest of my wishes now fulfilled—
What then—what then?

DAJA.

   What then? Then should I hope
My warmest wish might also be fulfilled.

RECHA.

What would supply the place within my breast,
Which swells no longer, uninspired by one
Supreme desire? What? Nothing? Ah, I tremble,

DAJA.

My wish shall take the place of yours fulfilled—
To know you are in Europe, and in hands
Deserving of you.

RECHA.

You're mistaken, Daja.
The motive that inspires that wish in you
Prevents it in myself. Your fatherland
Allures you; and shall mine, shall mine not hold
    me?
Shall images of home, unfaded yet
Within your soul, have greater power than home,
With all that I can see, and touch, and hear?

DAJA.

Resist with all your will—the ways of Heaven
Are still the ways of Heaven. How if through him
Who saved your life, his God for whom he fights
Would lead you to the land and to the people
For which your birth designed you?

RECHA.

        Daja, Daja!
What mean such words? What strange conceits
    you have!

"His God—for whom he fights!" Can God be
　　owned?
What sort of God were he whom man could own—
Who needs defenders? How can any tell
The spot of earth for which his birth designed
　　him,
If not the spot on which it placed him?—Daja,
What if my father heard such words from you!
What has he done that you should always paint
My happiness so far removed from him?
What has he done that you desire to mix
The seeds of understanding he has sown
So pure within my soul, with weeds or flowers
From your own distant land? You know, dear
　　Daja,
He'll none of your gay flowers upon my soil.
I, too, confess I feel my soil is weakened,
Exhausted by your flowers, e'en though they grace it;
And in their sweet, intoxicating fragrance
I grow bewildered, giddy. You, dear Daja,
Are more accustomed to it. No reproach
Upon the stronger nerves that can endure it;
Only it suits not me.—Your angel now;—
My head was well-nigh turned with it. I blush
E'en now, before my father, at such nonsense.

DAJA.

Nonsense! As if here only there were sense!
Oh, if I might but speak!

RECHA.

And may you not?
When was I not all ear to hear you tell
Of Christian heroes often as you would?
When gave I not their deeds my admiration,
Their sufferings my tears? True, their belief
I never held their greatest heroism;
But all the more consoling was the lesson
That faith in God depends not on the views
We entertain of Him. That has my father
So often told us; and yourself, dear Daja,
Have oft confirmed it. Why desire alone
To undermine what both have helped to build?—
But 'twere not well that we should meet our friend
With talk like this. And yet for me it is.
To me it matters infinitely whether—
Hark, Daja! Comes not some one to the door?
If it were he! Hark, hark!

SCENE II.

RECHA, DAJA, *and the* TEMPLAR, *for whom the door is opened, with the words* —"Be pleased to enter."

RECHA (*starts back, recovers herself, and is about to throw herself at his feet*).

'Tis he—'tis my preserver! Ah!

TEMPLAR.
　　　　　　　Thus late
I came to shun a scene like this ; and yet—

RECHA.

Here at the feet of this proud man, once more
Will I give thanks to God,—not to the man.
The man desires no thanks,—desires as little
As does the water-bucket, kept so busy
In putting out the flames.　'Twas filled and emptied
In total apathy.　So with the man.
Like that, he was but thrust into the fire ;
By accident I fell into his arms ;
There lay by accident within his arms,
E'en as a spark might lie upon his mantle,
Till something—what I know not—threw us both
Beyond the flames.　What cause for thanks in that?
Wine urges men to other deeds in Europe.—
'Twas but a Templar's duty.　They, like dogs
Of somewhat higher training, have to fetch
From fire as well as water.

TEMPLAR (*who has been gazing on her with surprise
and disquiet*).
　　　　　　Daja, Daja !
If moments of distress and bitterness
Had made me harsh with you, why bring to her
Each foolish word that might escape my lips ?
'Twas taking a too cruel vengeance, Daja.
Henceforth I hope for kindlier intercession.

DAJA.

Scarce think I, knight, these little stings of yours,
Flung at her heart, have harmed your cause with her,

RECHA.

Had you a grief, and were you of your grief
Less generous than of life ?

TEMPLAR.

Kind, gracious maiden !
How is my soul divided betwixt eye
And ear !   Not this the maiden that I saved—
It cannot, cannot be ; for who had known her
And not have saved her ? who would wait for me ?
'Tis true—that fear—deforms.

[*He pauses, lost in contemplation of her.*

RECHA.

Yet I find you
To be the same.

[*Another pause, until, to rouse him from his abstrac-
tion, she continues*]

But you must tell us, knight,
Where you have been so long.   Where are you now ?
I might almost have asked.

TEMPLAR.

I am, perhaps—
Where I ought not to be.

RECHA.

And where have been ?
Also, perhaps, where you should not have been?
That is not well.

TEMPLAR.

On—on—what is the mountain?
On Sinai.

RECHA.

Sinai ?   Ah, I'm glad ; for now
Can I learn surely if 'tis true—

TEMPLAR.

What—what?
If it be true that there the spot is shown
Where in God's presence Moses stood, when—

RECHA.

No ;
Not that. Where'er he stood, 'twas in God's presence.
Besides, I know enough of that already.
I only wanted you to tell me if—
If it were true there's much less weariness
In climbing up that mountain than descending.
With all the mountains I have ever climbed
'Twas just the contrary.—Well, knight, how now?
You turn away—you will not look at me !

TEMPLAR.

I would the better hear you.

RECHA.

You would hide
Your smiles at my simplicity,—your smiles
That no more worthy question can I ask
About that holy mountain,—would you not?

TEMPLAR.

Then must I look again into your eyes.
Ah, now you cast them down—conceal your smiles!
When I would read in features full of riddles
What I distinctly hear, will you disguise them?
Ah, Recha, truly said he, "Only know her!"

RECHA.

Who said—of whom—to you?

TEMPLAR.

Your father's words
To me in speaking of you—"Only know her!"

DAJA.

Did I not say it? Did not also I?

TEMPLAR.

But where is he, your father? Stays he yet
With Saladin?

RECHA.

No doubt.

TEMPLAR.

So long? Ah no:
Forgetful that I am! he's there no longer;

But by the convent yonder waits for me.
So, I am sure, it was agreed between us.
Permit me, I will go, will bring him.

DAJA.

        Nay;
Leave that to me.   Stay, stay, knight!   I will bring
  him
Without delay.

TEMPLAR.

    Not so, not so.   Myself,
Not you, is he expecting.   And, besides,
He may—who knows?—he may with Saladin—
You do not know the Sultan!—may perchance
Have met with difficulties.   There is danger,
Believe me, there is danger if I stay.

RECHA.

What danger?

TEMPLAR.

    Danger to myself, to you,
To him, unless I quickly, quickly go.   [*Goes.*

———

SCENE III.

RECHA *and* DAJA.

RECHA.

What means it, Daja?   Why so quick to leave us?
What sudden thought could thus have urged him off?

DAJA.

Let be—let be. I hold it no bad sign.

RECHA.

A sign—of what?

DAJA.

Something's astir within :
'Tis boiling, and must not be let boil over.
Let him alone. 'Tis your turn now.

RECHA.

My turn?
You're unintelligible, like himself.

DAJA.

Soon the disquietude he made you suffer
You can requite him. Only, show yourself
Not too severe, too unrelenting towards him.

RECHA.

I know not even of what you're talking, Daja.

DAJA.

So calm again?

RECHA.

I am ; indeed I am.

DAJA.

Confess at least that his disquietude
Rejoices you, and that to it you owe
Whate'er you have of calm.

- 9*

RECHA.

Not consciously.
The most I could confess would be my wonder
That suddenly the storm within my heart
Should be succeeded by so deep a stillness.
His whole appearance, conversation, bearing—

DAJA.

So soon have satisfied ?

RECHA.

Not satisfied.
No ; far from that—

DAJA.

But stilled your hungry longing ?

RECHA.

If you will have it so.

DAJA.

Not I indeed.

RECHA.

He will be always dear to me, far dearer
Than life itself ; though at his name my pulse
No longer varies, and my heart no longer
Beats harder, faster when I think of him.—
What nonsense am I talking?   Come, dear Daja,
We'll seek again the window toward the palms.

DAJA.

'Tis not then wholly stilled, that hungry longing.

RECHA.

Once more shall I behold the palms again;
Not only him beneath.

DAJA.

This coldness then
Portends new fever.

RECHA.

Coldness? I'm not cold.
With equal pleasure do I look, though calmly.

———

SCENE IV.

Audience hall in Saladin's palace. SALADIN. SITTAH.

SALADIN (*speaking to some one without as he enters*).
Admit the Jew the moment he arrives.
He's not disposed to hurry, it would seem.

SITTAH.

He was not there perhaps, in instant reach.

SALADIN.

O sister, sister!

SITTAH.

One would say a battle
Were threatening you.

SALADIN.

One to be waged with weapons
I never learned to use.   I must dissemble ;
Create uneasiness ; lay snares ; entice
On slippery ways.   When could I ever that ?
Where learned I ever that ?   And all for what—
For what ?   To fish for money—all for money !
To frighten money from a Jew—for money !
To such mean shifts am I reduced at last
To get the least of trifles !

SITTAH.

Every trifle,
Unduly scorned, will be revenged, dear brother.

SALADIN.

Alas, too true.   But now suppose this Jew
Should be the wise good man the dervise once
Described him.

SITTAH.

If he should !   Where lies the harm ?
The usurious, careful, timid Jew alone
The snare is laid for—not the wise, good man.
He without snares were ours.   What joy to hear
How such a man would extricate himself !
The downright force that would the meshes break,
Or crafty cunning that would disentangle—
This pleasure will be all to boot.

SALADIN.

That's true.
It were a joy indeed.

SITTAH.

There can arise
Naught further to disturb you.   Is he one
Of many—just a Jew like any Jew?
To such a one why be ashamed to seem
What he believes all men to be?   Nay, more;
Who should appear aught other, were to him
A fool, a dolt.

SALADIN.

I must act meanly, therefore,
Lest I be meanly thought of by the mean.

SITTAH.

If mean you call it, dealing with each thing
According to its nature.

SALADIN.

What contrivance
Of woman's brain will she not palliate !

SITTAH.

Not palliate?

SALADIN.

My clumsy hands, I fear,
Will break this keen and subtle thing.   It needs
To be conducted as 'twas first conceived,

With all dexterity and cunning.   Well,
I can but try !   I'll dance as best I may :
And yet would rather it were worse then better.

SITTAH.

Trust not yourself too little.   Do but will !
I'll answer for you.   See how men like you
Delight to make us think that with the sword,
The sword alone, you have achieved so much !
The lion is ashamed, if with the fox
He've hunted—of the fox, not of the craft.

SALADIN.

And how you women like to bring men down
To your own level !   Go, go ; leave me now ;
I know my lesson.

SITTAH.

           Leave you—must I go ?

SALADIN.

You had not thought to stay ?

SITTAH.

                If not to stay—
Not in your sight—yet in the adjoining room.

SALADIN.

That you may listen ?   If I'm to succeed,
That neither, sister.—Go ! the curtain stirs.
He comes !—Remain not near ; I'll see to it.

[*As she leaves by one door, Nathan enters by another,
and Saladin seats himself.*]

SCENE V.

SALADIN *and* NATHAN.

SALADIN.

Come nearer, Jew, come nearer!—without fear!

NATHAN.

'Tis for your foes to fear!

SALADIN.

Your name is Nathan?

NATHAN.

Yes.

SALADIN.

The wise Nathan?

NATHAN.

No.

SALADIN.

True, not the name
You give yourself, but that the people give you.

NATHAN.

May be.   The people!

SALADIN.

Think you I despise
The people's voice?   Long have I wished to know
The man they call the wise.

NATHAN.

If but in scorn
'They call him so; if to the people's thought
The wise is but the prudent, and the prudent
But he who understands his own advantage?

SALADIN.

His true advantage mean you?

NATHAN.

Then indeed
The selfish were the wise; then wise and prudent
Would be indeed the same.

SALADIN.

I hear you prove
What you would fain deny. Man's true advantage,
Mistaken by the people, is known to you;
Or has been sought by you; has been the theme
Of your reflections; that alone makes wise.

NATHAN.

Which every man esteems himself to be.

SALADIN.

Enough of modesty; it nauseates
To hear but that, when we expect dry reason.

                              [*Starts up.*

Let us to business. But be honest, Jew,—
Be honest!

NATHAN.

Sultan, I will surely serve you,
In manner to deserve your further custom.

SALADIN.

How serve me?

NATHAN.

You shall have the best of goods,
And at the lowest price.

SALADIN.

What speak you of—
Your merchandise? My sister presently
Will do the chaffering with you. (That for her,
The listener!) I've no business with the merchant.

NATHAN.

Then must you wish to learn what on my way
I may have seen, encountered of the foe,
Who is astir again ; if openly—

SALADIN.

Nor yet is that my present business with you.
Of that I know already all I need.—
In short—

NATHAN.

Command me, Sultan.

SALADIN.

I desire
Instruction of you in another matter—

10

In quite another.—Since so great your wisdom,
I pray you tell me what belief, what law
Has most commended itself to you.

NATHAN.
                              Sultan,
I am a Jew.

SALADIN.
              And I a Mussulman.
Between us is the Christian.   Now, but one
Of all these three religions can be true.
A man like you stands not where accident
Of birth has cast him.   If he so remain,
It is from judgment, reasons, choice of best.
Impart to me your judgment; let me hear
The reasons I've no time to seek myself.
Communicate, in confidence of course,
The choice you have arrived at through those reasons,
That I may make it mine.—You are surprised—
You weigh me with your glance!—May be that
    Sultan
Had ne'er such whim before; which yet I deem
Not unbecoming in a Sultan.   Speak—
Your answer!   Or a moment would you have
To think upon it?   Good; I grant it you.
(Can she be listening?   I'll surprise her then,
And learn if I've done well.)   But quick, be quick
With your reflections.   I'll not tarry long.
    [*Goes into the adjoining room, as Sittah had done.*

Scene VI.

Nathan (*alone*).

Hm!—singular indeed! What means it all?
What will the Sultan have? I am prepared
For money, and he asks for truth—for truth!
And wants it hard and bare, as truth were coin.
Yes; if an ancient coin which went by weight,
I grant you; but this coinage of to-day
That's counted down, and has no other value
Except the stamp upon it;—that she's not.
Can truth be swept into the head like gold
Into a sack? Which here is most the Jew—
Is't I or he?—But stay; what if the Sultan
Were not in earnest in his search for truth?
Nay; the suspicion he could use the truth
But for a snare, would be too mean. Too mean?
Is aught too mean for princes?—Surely, surely.
With what abruptness made he his attack!
One knocks and listens, if one comes as friend.—
I'll be upon my guard with him. But how?
To play the bigot Jew avails not here:
Still less no Jew at all. For if no Jew,
Well might he ask, why not a Mussulman?—
I have it,—that will save me; for with fables
Not children only can be entertained.
He comes: well, let him come!

Scene VII.

Saladin *and* Nathan.

Saladin.

                    (The coast is clear.)
I'm not returned too soon for you, I hope;
You've brought your meditations to a close?
Speak then ; no soul can hear us.

Nathan.

                         I am willing
The world should hear us.

Saladin.

                    Nathan is so sure
Of his good cause?   Ah, that I call a sage;
Never to hide the truth ; to stake on it
Your all ; your soul and body, goods and life.

Nathan.

When necessary it shall be, and useful.

Saladin.

With right I hope henceforth to bear my title,
Reformer of the world and of the law.

Nathan.

A noble title certainly.   Yet, Sultan,
Ere I bestow my perfect confidence,
Permit me to relate a story to you.

SALADIN.

Why not? I ever have been fond of stories
Well told.

NATHAN.

The telling well I do not promise.

SALADIN.

Again so proudly modest !—Come, your story !

NATHAN.

In gray antiquity there lived a man
In Eastern lands, who had received a ring —
Of priceless worth from a beloved hand.
Its stone, an opal, flashed a hundred colors,
And had the secret power of giving favor,
In sight of God and man, to him who wore it
With a believing heart. What wonder then
This Eastern man would never put the ring
From off his finger, and should so provide
That to his house it be preserved forever?
Such was the case. Unto the best-beloved
Among his sons he left the ring, enjoining
That he in turn bequeath it to the son
Who should be dearest ; and the dearest ever,
In virtue of the ring, without regard
To birth, be of the house the prince and head.
You understand me, Sultan?

SALADIN.

       Yes ; go on !
10*

NATHAN.

From son to son the ring descending, came
To one, the sire of three ; of whom all three
Were equally obedient ; whom all three
He therefore must with equal love regard.
And yet from time to time now this, now that,
And now the third,—as each alone was by,
The others not dividing his fond heart,—
Appeared to him the worthiest of the ring ;
Which then, with loving weakness, he would promise
To each in turn.   Thus it continued long.
But he must die ; and then the loving father
Was sore perplexed.   It grieved him thus to wound
Two faithful sons who trusted in his word ;
But what to do ?   In secrecy he calls
An artist to him, and commands of him
Two other rings, the pattern of his own ;
And bids him neither cost nor pains to spare
To make them like, precisely like to that.
The artist's skill succeeds.   He brings the rings,
And e'en the father cannot tell his own.
Relieved and joyful, summons he his sons,
Each by himself ; to each one by himself
He gives his blessing, and his ring—and dies.—
You listen, Sultan ?

SALADIN (*who, somewhat perplexed, has turned away*).

Yes ; I hear, I hear.
But bring your story to an end.

NATHAN.

'Tis ended ;
For what remains would tell itself. The father
Was scarcely dead, when each brings forth his ring,
And claims the headship. Questioning ensues,
Strife, and appeal to law ; but all in vain.
The genuine ring was not to be distinguished ;—
  [*After a pause, in which he awaits the Sultan's answer,*
As undistinguishable as with us
The true religion.

SALADIN.

That your answer to me ?

NATHAN.

But my apology for not presuming
Between the rings to judge, which with design
The father ordered undistinguishable.

SALADIN.

The rings ?—You trifle with me. The religions
I named to you are plain to be distinguished—
E'en in the dress, e'en in the food and drink.

NATHAN.

In all except the grounds on which they rest.
Are they not founded all on history,
Traditional or written ? History
Can be accepted only upon trust.
Whom now are we the least inclined to doubt?
Not our own people—our own blood ; not those

Who from our childhood up have proved their love;
Ne'er disappointed, save when disappointment
Was wholesome to us?   Shall my ancestors
Receive less faith from me, than yours from you?
Reverse it : Can I ask you to belie
Your fathers, and transfer your faith to mine?
Or yet, again, holds not the same with Christians?

SALADIN.

(By heaven, the man is right!   I've naught to answer.)

NATHAN.

Return we to our rings.   As I have said,
The sons appealed to law, and each took oath
Before the judge that from his father's hand
He had the ring,—as was indeed the truth ;
And had received his promise long before,
One day the ring, with all its privileges,
Should be his own,—as was not less the truth.
The father could not have been false to him,
Each one maintained ; and rather than allow
Upon the memory of so dear a father
Such stain to rest, he must against his brothers,
Though gladly he would nothing but the best
Believe of them, bring charge of treachery ;
Means would he find the traitors to expose,
And be revenged on them.

SALADIN.

And now the judge?
I long to hear what words you give the judge.
Go on !

NATHAN.

Thus spoke the judge : Produce your father
At once before me, else from my tribunal
Do I dismiss you.   Think you I am here
To guess your riddles ?   Either would you wait
Until the genuine ring shall speak ?—But hold !
A magic power in the true ring resides,
As I am told, to make its wearer loved—
Pleasing to God and man.   Let that decide.
For in the false can no such virtue lie.
Which one among you, then, do two love best ?
Speak !   Are you silent ?   Work the rings but
        backward,
Not outward ?   Loves each one himself the best ?
Then cheated cheats are all of you !   The rings
All three are false.   The genuine ring was lost ;
And to conceal, supply the loss, the father
Made three in place of one.

SALADIN.

Oh, excellent !

NATHAN.

Go, therefore, said the judge, unless my counsel
You'd have in place of sentence.   It were this :
Accept the case exactly as it stands.
Had each his ring directly from his father,
Let each believe his own is genuine.
'Tis possible your father would no longer
His house to one ring's tyranny subject ;

And certain that all three of you he loved,
Loved equally, since two he would not humble,
That one might be exalted.   Let each one
To his unbought, impartial love aspire ;
Each with the others vie to bring to light
The virtue of the stone within his ring ;
Let gentleness, a hearty love of peace,
Beneficence, and perfect trust in God,
Come to its help.   Then if the jewel's power
Among your children's children be revealed,
I bid you in a thousand, thousand years
Again before this bar.   A wiser man
Than I shall occupy this seat, and speak.
Go !—Thus the modest judge dismissed them.

SALADIN.

God !

NATHAN.

If therefore, Saladin, you feel yourself
That promised, wiser man—

SALADIN (*rushing to him, and seizing his hand, which
        he holds to the end*).

I ?   Dust !—I ?   Naught !

O God !

NATHAN.

What moves you, Sultan ?

SALADIN.

Nathan, Nathan !

Not ended are the thousand, thousand years

Your judge foretold ; not mine to claim his seat.
Go, go !—But be my friend.

NATHAN.

> No further orders

Has Saladin for me ?

SALADIN.

None.

NATHAN.

None ?

SALADIN.

> No, none.

Why ask ?

NATHAN.

> An opportunity I sought

To proffer a request.

SALADIN.

> Needs a request

An opportunity ?   Speak !

NATHAN.

> I'm returned

From distant journeyings to collect my debts.
Of ready money I've too much on hand.
Times grow again uncertain.   Scarce I know
Where safely to dispose it ; and I thought
That you, perhaps, since more is always needed
For an approaching war, might mine employ.

SALADIN (*fixing his eyes upon him.*)

I will not ask you, Nathan, if Al-Hafi
Has been already with you ;—will not ask
If no suspicion prompts this willing offer—

NATHAN.

Suspicion ?

SALADIN.

I deserve it ;—but forgive me !
Why seek to hide it ? Frankly, 'twas my purpose—

NATHAN.

Not to ask me the same ?

SALADIN.

It was indeed.

NATHAN.

Then can we both be served.   This Templar only
Prevents my sending you my whole supply.
You know the Templar.   I've a heavy debt
That first must be discharged to him.

SALADIN.

A Templar ?
You surely do not with your gold support
My bitterest foes ?

NATHAN.

I speak but of the one
Whose life you spared.

SALADIN.

What bring you to my mind !
The youth I'd utterly forgot.   You know him?
Where is he?

NATHAN.

Know you not how much your grace
Has flowed through him on me?   His new-found
    life
He risked to save my daughter from the fire.

SALADIN.

Ah, did he so?   He looked like such an one.
So had my brother done, whom he resembles.
Is he still here?   Conduct him hither to me.
So often have I spoken to my sister
Of this her brother whom she never knew,
She must behold his image.—Go, go find him !
From one good deed, though born of naught but
    passion,
How many other noble deeds will spring !
Go, find him !

NATHAN.

Instantly !—It stands agreed
About the other.   [*Goes.*

SALADIN.

Ah, why let I not
My sister listen?   To her, to her now !
How shall I ever tell her of it all ?

                    [*Goes out in the opposite direction.*

11

Scene VIII.

Grove of palms near the Convent, where the Templar
awaits Nathan.

Templar (*walking to and fro in conflict with himself,*
till he thus breaks forth).

Here must the weary victim cease his struggles.—
So be it then !   I will not, must not look
Into my heart more closely, nor forecast
The future for it.   Enough that flight was useless,
Useless.   And yet I could do nothing more
Than fly.—Now come what must !—Too suddenly
To be evaded fell at last the blow
That oft and long I had refused to meet.—
To see her, her I had so little wish
To see ; to see her, and resolve my eyes
Should never let her go— Resolve ?   Resolve
Is purpose, action.   I was simply passive.
To see her, and to feel my very being
Was linked with hers, bound up in hers forever,
Was instantaneous.   Life apart from her
Is inconceivable to me—were death ;
And wheresoe'er we may be after death,
There too were death.   If that be love, then—then—
The Templar loves—the Christian loves the Jewess.
What matter ?   Many a prejudice already

Have I discarded in the Holy Land—
Holy to me forever for that cause.
What will my Order further? I, the Templar,
Am dead. The moment I became the prisoner
Of Saladin, I died unto my Order.
This head the Sultan gave,—is it my old one?
Nay, 'tis a new one—one that has no knowledge
Of the traditions by which that was fettered.
A better too; and better calculated
To breathe my native air. That can I feel;
For it is giving me the very thoughts
My father must have cherished here before me,
Unless I've been imposed upon with fables.
Yet wherefore fables? Credible enough;
And never to my mind more credible
Than now, in danger as I am of stumbling
Where he has fallen.—Fallen? I will choose
Rather to fall with men than stand with children
His approbation is secured to me
By his example; and whose approbation
Could I desire besides? If Nathan's— Ah,
Still less can his encouragement be wanting—
Rather than approbation.—What a Jew!
Yet one who chooses to be thought a Jew,
And nothing better.—Here he comes in haste,
And glowing with delight, like all who come
From Saladin. Ho, Nathan!

Scene IX.

Nathan *and the* Templar.

NATHAN.

Is it you?

TEMPLAR.

You tarried long with Saladin.

NATHAN.

Less long
Than you imagine.   I was much delayed
In my departure.   Truly, truly, Curd,
The man is equal to his fame; his fame
Is but his shadow.   I must tell you first
And quickly—

TEMPLAR.

What?

NATHAN.

He will have speech with you;
Without delay he bids you to his presence.
First to my house with me, where his affairs
Demand my presence; then we'll go together.

TEMPLAR.

Your house I ne'er again will enter, Nathan,
Till—

NATHAN.

Have you been already—spoken with her?
Say, how does Recha please you?

TEMPLAR.

Past expression !
But never—never will I see her more !
Else must you promise it may be forever.

NATHAN.

How must I understand your words?

TEMPLAR (*after a pause, suddenly throwing himself on
Nathan's neck*).

My father !

NATHAN.

Young man !

TEMPLAR (*starting back from him as suddenly*).
Not son?—I pray you, Nathan !—

NATHAN.

Friend !

TEMPLAR.

Not son?—I pray you, Nathan !—I conjure you—
By Nature's earliest ties !   Let later bonds
Not take precedence of them !   Be content
To be a man !   Reject me not !

NATHAN.

Dear friend !

11*

TEMPLAR.

And son ?—not son ?— Not e'en if gratitude
Have in your daughter's heart prepared the way
For love—if both were waiting but your sign
To melt into each other !—You are silent ?

NATHAN.

You take me by surprise, young knight.

TEMPLAR.

Surprise ?
Surprise you with your own suggestions, Nathan ?
Sound they then unfamiliar from my lips ?
How take you by surprise ?

NATHAN.

Ere I e'en know
What Stauffen was your father ?

TEMPLAR.

Nathan, Nathan !
At such a moment have you no emotion
Save curiosity ?

NATHAN.

For in the past
A Stauffen well I knew : his name was Conrad.

TEMPLAR.

If 'twere my father's name ?

NATHAN.

Was it indeed ?

TEMPLAR.

I bear my father's name, Curd.   Curd is Conrad.

NATHAN.

My Conrad, though, could not have been your father;
For he was like yourself—he was a Templar ;
Ne'er married.

TEMPLAR

For that reason—

NATHAN.

What?

TEMPLAR.

For that

He might have been my father.

NATHAN.

You are jesting.

TEMPLAR.

And you are much too serious.   Where's the harm ?
A bit of bastard ; a bar sinister ;
A breed it is, no wise to be despised.—
But leave my ancestors unquestioned, Nathan ;
So shall your own go free.   No faintest doubt
I mean to cast upon your pedigree.
No ; God forbid !   You trace it, branch by branch,
As high as Abraham ; and from him still up
I know it well myself—could swear to it.

NATHAN.

You're bitter ; but have I deserved it from you ?

Have I yet aught refused? I would not hold you
Upon the instant to your word.   No more.

TEMPLAR.

No more?   Ah, then forgive !

NATHAN.

Come, come with me.

TEMPLAR.

And whither?—to your house? No, no; not there—
Not there !—it burns me !   I will wait you here.
Go.—If I am to look on her again,
'Twill be to gaze my fill ; if not—too much
Already have I seen her.

NATHAN.

I will haste.

——————

SCENE X.

THE TEMPLAR ; *soon afterwards* DAJA.

TEMPLAR.

More than enough !—how infinitely much
Man's brain will hold, and yet at times grows full
So suddenly,—so suddenly grows full
With naught !—Vain, vain—be it filled with what it
    may !—

But patience ! Soon upon this swollen mass
The soul will work, and space be cleared, and light
And order reign again.—Have I ne'er loved
Before? Was that not love, that love I deemed?
Can only this be love?

DAJA (*approaching stealthily*).

Knight, Knight!

TEMPLAR.

Who calls?

You, Daja?

DAJA.

Unperceived by him, I passed ;
Yet where you stand might he detect us. Come,
Come nearer me. This tree shall be our screen.

TEMPLAR

What is it? why so secret?

DAJA.

'Tis a secret
That brings me to you ; ay, a double secret ;
One known but to myself—one but to you.
What say you to exchanging? Give me yours,
And mine will I confide to you.

TEMPLAR.

Right gladly,
When first I know what you consider mine.
That doubtless shall I learn from yours. Begin!

DAJA.

Excuse me.   No, Sir Knight, you first; I follow.
Be sure my secret will avail you naught,
Have I not first your own.   Quick, therefore, quick!
Wait till I draw it from you, you will then
Have naught confided ; mine is still my own,
While yours is gone.—Poor Knight! that men should
     think
Such secrets can be hidden from a woman !

TEMPLAR.

Which oft we're quite unconscious of possessing.

DAJA.

'Tis possible.   Then will I kindly first
Acquaint you with your own. What meant it, Knight,
That with such headlong haste but now you fled ;
That you so left us wondering ; that with Nathan
You joined us not again ?   Made Recha, then,
So slight impression, or so great ?   So great !
So great !   The flutterings of the poor charmed bird
Chained to his perch, am I to learn from you ?
Come, own you love her, love her e'en to madness,
And I will tell you—

TEMPLAR.

               Madness ?   Truly, there
You speak of what you know.

DAJA.

                    Own then the love ;
I yield the madness.

TEMPLAR.

For it tells itself?
A Templar love a Jewess!

DAJA.

Little enough
Of reason seems there in it; yet have things
Ofttimes a deeper reason than we think.
No new thing were it that unto himself
The Saviour should conduct us upon ways
The wise would scarce have chosen.

TEMPLAR.

You are solemn,
(Yet if for Saviour read I Providence,
Is she not right?) My curiosity
Is stirred beyond its wont.

DAJA.

This is the land
Of wonders.

TEMPLAR.

(Of the wonderful indeed.
Could it be otherwise—since here the world
Is met together?) Take for granted, Daja,
Whatever you desire; say that I love her;
I cannot think of life without her; that—

DAJA.

In truth? Then swear to make her yours, to save her,
For time and for eternity to save her.

TEMPLAR.

How so—how can I so?   Can I then swear
What lies not in my power?

DAJA.

'Tis in your power.
One word of mine shall put it in your power.

TEMPLAR.

That e'en her father shall have naught against it?

DAJA.

Oh, never mind the father!   He must yield.

TEMPLAR.

Must, Daja?   Has he fallen among thieves?
There is no must.

DAJA.

Well, well; he must be willing—
He must be glad at last.

TEMPLAR.

He must—and glad?
If I should tell you, Daja, 'tis a chord
I've struck already!

DAJA.

And he chimed not in?

TEMPLAR.

He answered with a discord that offended.

DAJA.

What say you? At the shadow of a wish
You showed for Recha, leaped he not for joy,
But drew with coldness back, raised difficulties?

TEMPLAR.

'Twas nearly so.

DAJA.

Then not one moment more
I hesitate.

TEMPLAR.

Yet still you hesitate?

DAJA.

So good he is in all besides! my debt
To him so great! Oh that he would but hear!
God knows my heart is bleeding thus to force him.

TEMPLAR.

I pray you keep me not in this suspense!
Yet if yourself uncertain whether good
Or evil, culpable or laudable
Your purpose, speak not. I'll forget there's aught
To be concealed.

DAJA.

That checks me not, but spurs me.
Know then that Recha is no Jewish maiden;
She is—a Christian.

TEMPLAR (*coldly*).

I congratulate you.

12

Found you the labor hard ?   Let not the throes
Dismay you !   Still continue zealously
To people heaven, when you can naught for earth.

DAJA.

How, Knight ! Deserves my confidence your scorn !
Care you—you, Christian, Templar, Lover too—
Care you so little Recha is a Christian ?

TEMPLAR.

Especially a Christian of your making !

DAJA.

You take me so ?   No wonder then !   Not so ;
I'd like to see who could convert her !   No !
It is her happiness to have been long
What she is spoiled forever for becoming.

TEMPLAR.

Tell all, or—go !

DAJA.

                She is a Christian child ;
Of Christian parents born ; baptized—

TEMPLAR (*hastily*).

                                And Nathan ?

DAJA.

Is not her father !

TEMPLAR.

                Nathan not her father !
Know you what you are saying ?

DAJA.
The truth which oft
Has cost me tears of blood.—He's not her father !

TEMPLAR.

But as his daughter brought her up ?   A Christian
Brought up as Jewess ?

DAJA.
Yes.

TEMPLAR.
And knows she not
What she was born ? ne'er has she learned from him
That she was born a Christian, not a Jewess ?

DAJA.

Never.

TEMPLAR.

Not only did he train the child
In this delusion, but in this delusion
Allow the maid to rest ?

DAJA.
Alas, too true !

TEMPLAR.

Could Nathan, wise and good, allow himself
The voice of Nature thus to falsify ;
Thus misdirect the emotions of a heart
Which of themselves had flowed in other channels?
A something you indeed have told me, Daja,

Which is of weight ; is big with consequences ;
Bewilders me ; throws doubt upon my course.—
I must have time.   Go !   He will come this way,
And might surprise us.   Go !

DAJA.

> Ah, that were death !

TEMPLAR.

I am unfit to meet him.   If you see him,
Say that before the Sultan he shall find me.

DAJA.

No hint to him !   Reserve that till the last,
To take from you all scruples touching Recha.
But when you take her back to Europe, Knight,
Pray, leave me not behind.

TEMPLAR.

> We'll see.   Go, go !

ACT FOURTH.

Scene I.

The cloisters of the Monastery. The Lay-brother; *afterwards the* Templar.

Lay-brother.

Ay, ay; the Patriarch's in the right; 'tis true,
Of all the matters he intrusted to me,
Not many would succeed.   But why intrust
Such matters to me?   I've no knack at plotting,
Persuading, thrusting everywhere my nose,
In every dish my fingers.   But for this
Did I forsake the world, to be involved
More deeply in it by affairs of others?

Templar (*approaching him hurriedly*).
You're here, good brother! I have sought you long.

Lay-brother.
Me, Knight?

Templar.
Have you so soon forgotten me?

Lay-brother.
Not so; I only thought that ne'er in life
Would further sight of you be granted me;

12*

And hoped to Heaven it never might. God knows
How much I loathed my errand to the Knight:
He knows if ready ear I hoped to find ;
Knows how I was rejoiced, at heart rejoiced,
That you would give it scarce a thought, but flatly
Rejected what would ill become a knight.—
But now you seek me. It has taken effect.

TEMPLAR.

You know why I am come? I scarce could tell.

LAY-BROTHER.

You have considered it; find, after all,
The Patriarch not so wrong ; that fame and fortune
Lie in his offer ; that a foe's a foe,
Though he had been seven times our angel. That,
All that, with flesh and blood you've balanced well,
And come and offer for the work. Alas !

TEMPLAR.

Good man, take comfort : not for that I come ;
Not therefore do I seek the Patriarch.
His offer do I still esteem as then.
For all the world could give, I would not lose
The approval once vouchsafed me by a man
So honest, kind, and true. I only come
To ask the Patriarch's counsel in a matter—

LAY-BROTHER.

The Patriarch's? Seeks a knight a priest's—
            [*Casting a frightened look around.*

TEMPLAR.
Yes, brother ;
The case is somewhat priestly.

LAY-BROTHER.
Ne'er would priest
Consult a knight, the case be e'er so knightly.

TEMPLAR.
For 'tis the priest's prerogative to err :
One we'll not greatly envy him.   Indeed,
Concerned this matter but myself alone,
Were I but to myself accountable,
What need of Patriarch ?   But some things there are
I'd rather do amiss by others' judgment,
Than wisely by my own.   Besides, I've learned
Religion also is a party thing ;
The most impartial, as he deems himself,
Defends unconsciously his favorite side.—
Since so it is, we must suppose it right.

LAY-BROTHER.
I would be silent—understanding not
The Knight.

TEMPLAR.
And yet—(what is it here I want—
Decree or counsel ?—counsel plain or learned ?)
Thanks, brother, for the hint.   Why Patriarch ?
Be you my Patriarch ; for it is the Christian
Within the Patriarch that I would consult,
And not the Patriarch in the Christian.   Listen !

LAY-BROTHER.

No further, Knight—no further ! To what purpose?
The Knight mistakes me. He who has much know-
    ledge
Has many cares, and I am pledged to one.
But see—he comes himself, most happily.
Wait where you are ; already he has seen you.

———

SCENE II.

The PATRIARCH *advancing in great pomp on one side of
the cloisters, and the preceding.*

TEMPLAR.

I would I could escape. He's not my man !
A red, fat, jolly prelate ; and what state !

LAY-BROTHER.

See him arrayed for court ! Now he but comes
From visiting the sick.

TEMPLAR.

        How Saladin
Must blush before him !

        PATRIARCH (*signs to the Brother*).

              Here !—I see the Templar.
What will he have ?

LAY-BROTHER.

I know not.

PATRIARCH (*approaching the Templar, while the brother and attendants fall back*).

Ah, Sir Knight—
Most glad so gallant a young man to greet;
Ay, still so young! Great things will come of you,
God helping.

TEMPLAR.

Scarcely greater, reverend Sir,
Than what have come; more likely somewhat less.

PATRIARCH.

I hope at least a knight so pious may bloom
And flourish long, an honor and a gain
To Christendom and to the cause of God;
Which cannot fail if, wisely, youthful daring
Will use the ripe experience of age.
How can I serve the Knight?

TEMPLAR.

By giving that
In which my youth is wanting—counsel.

PATRIARCH.

Gladly,
Provided, only, counsel will be taken.

TEMPLAR.

Not blindly, certainly?

PATRIARCH.

I say not blindly.
No man indeed should fail to use the reason
That God has given him—in its proper place.
But is that everywhere? Oh no! For instance :
Should God vouchsafe to show us by an angel—
That is, a servant of His holy word—
A means of furthering, establishing
The welfare of all Christendom, the good
Of Holy Church in an especial manner,
Who would presume to let his reason question
The absolute authority of Him
Who made that reason—try the eternal law
Of Heaven's high majesty by narrow rules
Of idle honor? But enough of this.
Now on what question seeks the Knight our counsel?

TEMPLAR.

Suppose, most reverend Father, that a Jew
Should have an only child, an only daughter—
Trained up in every virtue by his care,
Loved more than his own soul, who, in return,
Loves him with fond devotion—and 'twere told
To one of us the girl was not his daughter ;
That he had bought, found, stolen her, what you will,
In childhood ; and that further it was known
She was a Christian, and had been baptized,—
The Jew had only brought her up a Jewess,
Would only have her taken for a Jewess,

And his own daughter.   Say, most reverend Father,
How shall such case be dealt with?

PATRIARCH.
Ah, I shudder!
First let the Knight explain if this be fact
Or but hypothesis; that is to say,
If he invented it, or if 'twere done,
Be doing now.

TEMPLAR.
That deem I unimportant;
I would but learn your Reverence's opinion.

PATRIARCH.
Deem unimportant!   There the Knight may see
How pride of human reason will mislead
In matters spiritual.   Not unimportant;
For is the case proposed a play of wit,
It merits not my serious reflection.
I should refer the Knight to any theatre
Where with applause the pros and cons are argued.
But if the Knight put no stage trick upon me;
If this be fact; if in our diocese,
In our dear city of Jerusalem,
It shall have come to pass; then—

TEMPLAR.
And what then?

PATRIARCH.
Then should be executed on the Jew,
Without delay, the penalty decreed

Against such crimes, such outrages, by laws
Imperial and papal.

TEMPLAR.

So ?

PATRIARCH.

Those laws
Decree to any Jew who from the faith
A Christian shall pervert, the stake—the flames—

TEMPLAR.

So ?

PATRIARCH.

How much more to one who shall have torn
By violence from her baptismal vows
A Christian child !   For all is violence
That's done to children, is it not?—that is,
Excepting what the Church may do to children.

TEMPLAR.

But if the child in misery had died,
Unless the Jew had had compassion on it ?

PATRIARCH.

It matters not ; the Jew goes to the stake !
Better the child had died in misery here
Than thus be saved for everlasting ruin.—
Besides, why need the Jew anticipate
God's providence ?   Without him God can save,
If save he will.

TEMPLAR.

And e'en in spite of him,
I trow, accord salvation.

PATRIARCH.

Matters not ;
The Jew goes to the stake !

TEMPLAR.

I grieve to hear it.
The more because the girl is trained, 'tis said,
In no religion rather than his own ;
And has been taught no more nor less of God
Than satisfies her reason.

PATRIARCH.

Matters not ;
The Jew goes to the stake !—a triple stake,
For that alone he'd merit.   Let a child
Grow up with no religion—teach it naught
Of the important duty of believing !
That is too much !   I marvel, Knight, that you—

TEMPLAR.

The rest in the confessional, God willing,
Most reverend Sir.   [*About to go.*

PATRIARCH.

You give no explanation ?
You name me not this criminal, this Jew ?
Produce him not ?   But I have means at hand.

13

I'll instantly to Saladin.   The Sultan,
According to the treaty he has sworn,
Must, must protect us ; in the rights, the doctrines
That for the true religion we may claim,
He must protect us.   The original,
Thank God, is ours.   We have his hand and seal.
'Twere easy to convince him, too, the State,
By this believing nothing, is endangered ;
All hold upon the citizen dissolved,
When he's permitted to believe in nothing.
Away with such a scandal !

TEMPLAR.

               I regret
Not having greater leisure to enjoy
So excellent a sermon.   Saladin
Has summoned me.

PATRIARCH.

            The Sultan ?—Then—indeed—

TEMPLAR.

I will, if it shall please your Reverence,
Prepare the Sultan.

PATRIARCH.

           Ah !—The Knight, I know,
Found favor with the Sultan.   I but pray
To be remembered favorably to him.
My only motive is my zeal for God.
If I in aught exceed, 'tis for his sake.

I pray the Knight will so consider it.
That tale about the Jew was but a problem—
Not so, Sir Knight? That is to say—

TEMPLAR.

A problem. [*Goes.*

PATRIARCH.

(Yet one that must be sifted to the bottom.
Another excellent commission that
For brother Bonafides.)—Here, my son !
[*Speaks on his way out with the Lay-brother.*

SCENE III.

*A room in the Sultan's palace. A number of slaves
bring in bags and lay them side by side upon the floor.*
SALADIN ; *soon afterwards* SITTAH.

SALADIN (*entering*).

What ! 'Tis not ended yet ! Is much remaining ?

SLAVE.

As much again.

SALADIN.

Then take the rest to Sittah.—
Where tarries Hafi ? Hafi should be here
To take immediate charge of this. Or were it
Not better carried to my father ? Here

It will but slip away from me.   'Tis true,
One's heart grows hard at last ; and surely now
'Twould take some skill to squeeze much out of me.
At least, until the moneys come from Egypt,
The poor must make what shift they can.—The alms
About the sepulchre, if only they
Might be continued ; if the Christian pilgrims
Need only not go empty-handed ; if—

SITTAH.

What means all this ?   Why all this gold for me ?

SALADIN.

Repay yourself from it, and lay up store,
If any's over.

SITTAH.

Nathan not yet come
With the young Templar ?

SALADIN.

He is everywhere
In search of him.

SITTAH.

See what I found but now,
While searching 'mongst my jewels.
                    [*Showing him a miniature.*

SALADIN.

Ha !   My brother !
'Tis he—'tis he !   Was he—was he !   Alas !

My noble boy! oh, why so early lost!
What might I not have done, with you beside me?
Leave me the picture, Sittah.   Well I know it.
He gave it to your sister, to his Lilla,
One morning when she hung about his neck,
And would not let him go.   It was the last
He rode abroad.   I let him go—alone.
Poor Lilla died of grief, and ne'er forgave me
That I should let him thus ride forth alone.—
He came not back.

SITTAH.

Poor brother!

SALADIN.

Be it so!
One day we all shall go and come not back.—
Besides—who knows— Not death alone defeats
The hopes of such as he.   More foes he has;
And oft the strongest yields him like the weakest.
But be it as it may!—The Templar's face
I must compare with this;—must read in this
How far my fancy has misled me.

SITTAH.

Yes;
For that I brought it here.   But give it me!
I'll tell you best; a woman's eye sees quicker.

SALADIN (*to an attendant who enters*).

Who's there?   If 'tis the Templar, bid him enter.

13*

SITTAH.

That you be not disturbed, nor he confused
By my examination—
[*Seats herself upon a sofa, her face partly averted,
and drops her veil.*

SALADIN.

That is well!
(Now for his voice—how will it be with that?
The tones of Assad slumber still within me.)

———

SCENE IV.

The TEMPLAR *and* SALADIN.

TEMPLAR.

Your prisoner, Sultan—

SALADIN.

Prisoner? Grant I life,
And grant not freedom too?

TEMPLAR.

What you may grant
'Tis mine to learn, and not anticipate.
But, Sultan, thanks to offer for my life
Accords not with my character or Order.
At any call that life is at your service.

SALADIN.

I ask you but to use it not against me.
My foe I grudge not one more pair of hands ;
But 'twould go hard one more such heart to give him.
I've been in naught deceived in you, young man—
You're Assad o'er again in form and soul.
Yea, I might ask you where through all these years
You've been in hiding ; sleeping in what cave ;
What kindly power, within what Ginnistan,
Has kept my flower from year to year so fresh.
I might attempt to call up memories
Of what we did together here or there ;
Might chide you that you kept one secret from me ;
Excluded me from one adventure.   Yes,
That might I if I look not at myself,
But only you.—Enough.   Of these sweet dreams
So much at least is true, that in my autumn
An Assad is to bloom for me again.
Consent you, Knight?

TEMPLAR.

Whatever comes from you
Already lay, a wish, within my heart.

SALADIN.

That test we on the instant.   Stay with me,
About me.   As a Mussulman or Christian,
Alike to me !   In turban or in hat,
White cloak or Turkish mantle—as you will !
I ne'er required one bark on every tree.

TEMPLAR.

Else were you not, as now you are, the hero,
Who fain would be God's husbandman.

SALADIN.
                                   So then,
If thus you judge me, we are half agreed.

TEMPLAR.

Quite !

SALADIN (*offering his hand*).

Done ?

TEMPLAR (*grasping it*).

A bargain !   More receive with this
Than you could force from me.   I'm wholly yours !

SALADIN.

Too much to gain in one short day—too much !
Came *he* not with you here ?

TEMPLAR.

Who ?

SALADIN.

Nathan.

TEMPLAR (*coldly*).
                                   No ;

I came alone.

SALADIN.

Yours was a noble deed ;

And what a happy chance that such a deed
Should work the good of such a man !

TEMPLAR.

Oh yes.

SALADIN.

So coldly ?   Nay, young man, be not so cold
When you are made God's instrument for good ;
Nor wish through modesty so cold to seem.

TEMPLAR.

Why are all things on earth so many-sided,
And all their sides so hard to reconcile !

SALADIN.

Hold always to the best, and give God thanks.
'Tis His to reconcile them.   But, young man,
If you will be so difficult, I too
Must be upon my guard with you.   I too,
Alas, have many sides which oft seem hard
To reconcile.

TEMPLAR.

You pain me ; for suspicion
Is scarce among my faults.

' SALADIN.

Whom, then, suspect ?
Nathan, it seems ; but how ?   Nathan suspected ?
Explain ; give your first proof of confidence.

TEMPLAR.

Naught have I against Nathan ; with myself
I'm angry.

SALADIN.

And for what ?

TEMPLAR.

For having dreamed
That Jew could e'er be aught but Jew ; that waking
I should have dreamed.

SALADIN.

Out with your waking dream !

TEMPLAR.

Of Nathan's daughter you have heard.   The deed
I did for her, I did—because I did it.
Too proud to reap the thanks I had not sowed,
I haughtily refused from day to day
To see the girl.   The father was away :
But he returns ; he hears ; he seeks me out ;
He thanks me ; hopes that I may like his daughter ;
He talks of happy prospects for the future.
And I allow myself to be persuaded ;
Go, see her, find indeed a maiden— Ah,
I must take shame upon me, Sultan.

SALADIN.

Shame ?
Because a Jewish maiden charmed you ?   Never.

TEMPLAR.

Because my over-hasty heart, misled
By Nathan's flattering words, scarce made resistance.
Oh fool ! again I sprang into the flames ;
For now I sued, and now was I disdained.

SALADIN.

Disdained ?

TEMPLAR.

Not utterly did he reject me,
The cautious father : but he must consider ;
Must make inquiries.   Did I not the same?
Did I not first consider and inquire,
When she was shrieking in the flames ?   By heaven !
A noble thing to be so wise, so cautious !

SALADIN.

Nay ; be indulgent to his years ! How long
Will his refusal hold ? till you turn Jew ?

TEMPLAR.

Who knows ?

SALADIN.

Who knows ?   He who reads Nathan better.

TEMPLAR.

That superstition which has grown with us,
Know it for superstition though we may,
Relaxes not for that its hold upon us.
Not all who scorn their chains are free.

SALADIN.

Well said ;
But Nathan—

TEMPLAR.

'Tis the worst of superstitions
To deem one's own the most endurable.

SALADIN.

That may be so ; but Nathan—

TEMPLAR.

As the one
In which alone purblind humanity
May trust, till it can bear the clearer day
Of truth ; the only one—

SALADIN.

Well, well ; but Nathan !
Such weakness cannot be the doom of Nathan.

TEMPLAR.

So thought I too ; but if this paragon
Were so the common Jew, that Christian children
He seeks to gain, to bring them up as Jews—
What then ?

SALADIN.

Who is it brings such charge against him ?

TEMPLAR.

That very maiden he decoyed me with,
With hope of whom he seemed so glad to pay

The service I was not to be allowed
To render her for nothing ;—she herself
Is not his daughter, but a Christian child
Lost to her faith.

SALADIN.

Whom yet he could refuse you?

TEMPLAR.

Refuse or not, I have discovered him !
This tolerant pretender is exposed !
I'll set upon the track of this Jew wolf
In his sheep's clothing of philosophy,
Hounds that shall tear and worry.

SALADIN (*sternly*).

Christian, peace !

TEMPLAR.

Peace, Christian, peace ! What? Mussulman and
    Jew
Are to insist on Mussulman and Jew,
And only Christians must not act the Christian ?

SALADIN (*more sternly*).

Peace, Christian, peace !

TEMPLAR.

Ay, fully do I feel

The burden of reproach that Saladin
Compresses in those words.—If I but knew
How Assad would have done, had he been here !

14

SALADIN.

But little better ; just as violent.
Who taught you thus to bribe me with a word,
Like him ?   Indeed, if what you tell be true,
I have been disappointed in this Nathan.—
Still he's a friend : ne'er must one friend of mine
Have quarrel with another.—Be advised ;
Move cautiously ; denounce him not in haste
To your fanatics ; rather hide a deed
Your priesthood would appeal to me to avenge.
Be not a Christian to the injury
Of Jew or Mussulman.

TEMPLAR.

                    Almost too late !
Thanks to the Patriarch's eagerness for blood
I shrank from being his tool.

SALADIN.

                    Ere seeking me
You sought the Patriarch ?

TEMPLAR.

                    In the storm of passion,
The whirl of doubt !   Forgive !   No more of Assad
Will you acknowledge in me now, I fear.

SALADIN.

That very fear !   Methinks I know the faults
From which our virtue grows.   Cherish but this,

And those shall not weigh heavily against you.
But go ; seek Nathan as he sought for you,
And bring him hither.   I must clear away
All difference between you.   Are you earnest
About the maiden, 'be at rest.   She's yours ;
And Nathan pays the penalty for keeping
A Christian child from eating pork.   Now go !

Scene V.

Saladin *and* Sittah.

Sittah.

Most wonderful !

Saladin.

Confess, a handsome boy
My Assad must have been.

Sittah.

If it be he
The picture represents, and not the Templar.
But how could you forget to learn his parents?

Saladin.

And chief, his mother—if his mother e'er
Were in our land—not so ?

Sittah.

It were well done.

SALADIN.

Naught likelier; for such a favorite
Was Assad with the beauteous Christian ladies,
Was of the Christian ladies so enamored,
The story ran— Nay, best not speak of it.
Enough, I have him back; with all his faults,
With all the fancies of his too fond heart,
Will have him back.   O Sittah, must not Nathan
Give him the maiden?

SITTAH.

Give her?   Leave her to him !

SALADIN.

True; for what right has Nathan over her,
If he be not her father?   Who preserved
Her life, alone can claim the rights of him
Who gave it.

SITTAH.

How if you should place the maiden
Beneath your own protection, Saladin—
At once withdraw her from her wrongful keeper?

SALADIN

Would that be necessary?

SITTAH,

Necessary
Indeed 'tis not; my curiosity
Alone suggests the counsel.   There are men
Of whom I'd know at once what girl they love.

SALADIN.

Send for her then.

SITTAH.

Have I permission, brother?

SALADIN. •

Spare Nathan only; Nathan must not think
We want to force her from him.

SITTAH.

Have no fear.

SALADIN.

And I myself must learn what keeps Al-Hafi.

———

SCENE VI.

*The open court of Nathan's house, looking toward the
palms, as in first scene of first act. Some of the
wares therein mentioned are lying about unpacked.*
NATHAN *and* DAJA.

DAJA.

Oh, all is beautiful—all exquisite!
All—such as only you could give. Whence came
That silver stuff with golden vines upon it?
How costly was it?—That's a wedding-dress!
No queen could want a better.

14*

NATHAN.
                          Wedding-dress !
Why wedding-dress ?

DAJA.
            That was not in your mind
When you were buying ; but that it must be, Nathan ;
No other one than that.   'Tis as 'twere made
To grace a bridal.   See ; the ground of silver,
A type of innocence ; the golden streams
That twine themselves in all directions on it,
A type of riches.   Perfect, is it not ?

NATHAN.
What fancies are you weaving ?   Whose the dress
That you're so learnedly interpreting ?
Are you the bride ?

DAJA.
        I ?

NATHAN.
Who then ?

DAJA.
                    I ?   Good heavens !

NATHAN.
Who then ? Whose wedding-dress? All this is yours,
Yours only.

DAJA.
        Mine ?   All meant for me—not Recha ?

NATHAN.

Another bale holds those I brought for Recha.
Away with them ! off with your silken stuffs !

DAJA.

No, tempter ; all the treasures of the world
I would not touch, unless you swear to me
This single opportunity to seize,
Whose like heaven scarce a second time will grant.

NATHAN.

How seize ?—the opportunity for what ?

DAJA.

Feign not such ignorance !—In short, the Templar
Loves Recha.   Give her to him.   Thus your sin,
Whose secret I can keep for you no longer,
Is ended ; Recha is restored to Christians—
Becomes herself again—will be again
What at the first she was ; and all your kindness,
For which no words can give you fitting thanks,
Heaps coals of fire no more upon your head.

NATHAN.

The same old story to another tune,
For which, I fear, it has no sense or measure.

DAJA.

How so ?

NATHAN.

Against the Templar have I naught.

Rather to him than any in the world
Would I give Recha.   But—you must have patience

DAJA.

Patience ! that's your old story o'er again.

NATHAN.

Yet a few days have patience.—See, who comes ?
A brother from the convent ?   Ask his pleasure.

DAJA.

What can he want ?

[*She approaches and questions him.*

NATHAN.

Give—and before he asks.—
(Could I approach the Knight, yet tell him not
The motive of my curiosity !
Were that revealed and my suspicion false,
Then has my fatherhood been risked in vain.)
What is it ?

DAJA.

He would speak with you.

NATHAN.

Admit him ;
And leave us.

SCENE VII.

NATHAN *and the* LAY-BROTHER.

NATHAN.

(Would that Recha's father still
I might remain !—Why can I not, e'en though
Without the name ?—That she herself would give,
Did she but know how gladly I would own it.)
What can I do to serve you, brother ?

LAY-BROTHER.

                                    Little.—
I'm glad to see that Nathan keeps in health.

NATHAN.

You know me then ?

LAY-BROTHER.

              Who knows you not ?   Your name
Has been imprinted in too many hands.
For many years has it been writ in mine.

NATHAN (*feeling for his purse*).

Come, brother, come ; let me refresh it.

LAY-BROTHER.

                                    Thanks !
I take no alms ; 'twere stealing from the poorer.—
With your permission, I'd refresh in you

The imprint of my own ; for I can boast
That in your hand a thing of no small value
By me was laid.

NATHAN.

Your pardon—I am shamed !
ᴧay what it was, and take seven times its worth
As an atonement.

LAY-BROTHER.

Hark, while I shall tell
How first to-day the memory of that trust
By me confided to you was awakened.

NATHAN.

Trust you confided me ?

LAY-BROTHER.

Not long ago,
On Quarantana, near to Jericho,
I dwelt—a hermit.   Arab robbers came,
Destroyed my cell and little house of God,
And took me captive ; but I happily
Escaped their hands, ɪnd to the Patriarch
I hither fled to beg another place,
Where I might serve my God in solitude
Until my blessed end.

NATHAN.

I'm on the rack,
Good brother.   Make it brief !   The trust—the trust
Confided to me !

LAY-BROTHER.

Yet a moment, Nathan.
The earliest vacant hermitage on Tabor
The Patriarch promised me, and bade me stay
Meanwhile within the convent as a brother.
There am I now, and hundred times a day
I long for Tabor ; for the Patriarch
Puts every loathsome errand on me.   Thus—

NATHAN.

Be quick, I pray you.

LAY-BROTHER.

This is it.—A Jew,
So some one whispered in his ear to-day,
Is living here among us, who has trained
A Christian child as she had been his daughter.

NATHAN (*amazed*).

What?

. LAY-BROTHER.

Hear me out !—When he commissions me
To ferret out this Jew without delay,
No matter where ; and flies into a passion
Against so black a crime, which he esteems
The very sin against the Holy Ghost—
The sin, that is, which of all other sins
Brings greatest guilt upon us ; though, thank God,
We know not well in what that sin consists—
Then suddenly my conscience was awakened ;
The thought arose that possibly myself,

In years gone by, had furnished the occasion
For this unpardonable sin.   For say,
Did not a groom deliver to your care,
Some eighteen years ago, an infant child?

NATHAN.

How say you ?—'Twas indeed—yes, surely—

LAY-BROTHER.

Nathan.

Look at me well !—That groom was I !

NATHAN.

Was you?

LAY-BROTHER.

The Knight from whom I brought it you was named,
If I mistake not, Filneck—Wolf von Filneck.

NATHAN.

You're right.

LAY-BROTHER.

The mother had but lately died ;
The father unexpectedly was forced
To make retreat on—Gazza, as I think,
Where the poor baby could not follow him,
And so was sent to you.   'Twas in Darun,
I think, we found you.

NATHAN.
Right !

LAY-BROTHER.

It were no wonder
If memory played me false ; so many masters
I've served, and this one for too brief a season.
At Askalon soon afterward he fell.
A man to love he was.

NATHAN.

He was indeed.
How many, many services I owe him !
He more than once preserved me from the sword.

LAY-BROTHER.

Good ; all the readier must you then have been
To adopt his little child.

NATHAN.

You may believe it !

LAY-BROTHER.

Where is she, then ?   She surely is not dead !
Grant she may not have died !   If no one else
Have learned her story, then will all be well.

NATHAN.

You think so ?

LAY-BROTHER.

Trust me, Nathan ; thus I argue :
If close beside the good which I propose
Great evil lurk, I leave the good undone ;
Since of the evil can be little doubt,

But of the good there's much.   'Twas natural
If you would train the Christian's daughter well,
To train her as your own.—This have you done
In love and truth—but to be so rewarded?
I'll not believe it.—Wiser had it been
The Christian to have trained at second-hand
A Christian ; but you would not then have loved
The little daughter of your friend ; and children
Need love, though but a wild beast's love it be,
In those first years, above Christianity.
Christianity will still find time enough.
Have but the child in health and innocence
Grown up before your eyes, in sight of God
She's as she was.—Has not Christianity
Its root in Judaism ?   It oft has vexed,
Provoked me e'en to tears, to see how Christians
Forget our Saviour was himself a Jew.

NATHAN.

Good Brother, you must intercede for me
When hatred and hypocrisy shall rise
Against me for a deed—ah, for a deed—
You, you alone shall know it.   Bear it with you—
Into your grave.   Ne'er yet has vanity
Seduced me into telling it to man.
I tell it only to yourself.   I tell it
To pious simplicity alone ; for that
Alone can know what victories over self
Are possible to the devout believer.

LAY-BROTHER.

Your heart is stirred ; the tears are in your eyes !

NATHAN.

You found me at Darun—the child and you.
You did not know that Christians just before
Had murdered all the Jews that were in Gath—
Men, women, children ; knew not that my wife
And sons, seven hopeful sons, were there among
    them,
And in my brother's house, where they had fled
For safety, had to perish in the flames.

LAY-BROTHER.

All-gracious God !

NATHAN.

           Three days and nights I'd lain
In dust and ashes before God, and wept
When you arrived. Wept ? I had wrestled hard
At times with God ; had stormed and raved ; had
    cursed
Myself and all the world ; had sworn a hate
Against the Christians, unappeasable.

LAY-BROTHER.

I can believe it !

NATHAN.

           Gradually my reason
Returned to me. She spoke with gentle voice :
"And yet God is : e'en this was God's decree !

Up, then ! and practise what you've long believed.
To practise cannot be more difficult
Than to believe, if you but will.   Rise up !"
I stood erect and cried to God : "I will !
Oh, will Thou that I will !"—Dismounting then,
You handed me the child, wrapped in your cloak.
All that you said to me, or I to you,
Has been forgot.   I know but this : I took
The child ; I laid it on my bed ; I kissed it ;
I threw myself upon my knees, and sobbed,
"O God ! of seven, Thou grantest me one again !"

LAY-BROTHER.

You are a Christian, Nathan !   Yes, by heaven,
You are a Christian !   Never was a better !

NATHAN.

What makes of me a Christian in your eyes,
Makes you in mine a Jew.—Happy for both !
But let us not unman each other longer.
This calls for deeds.—Although a sevenfold love
Soon bound me to this lonely stranger girl—
Although the thought of losing all my sons
Again in her is death—if Providence
Should claim her back from me, I will obey.

LAY-BROTHER.

That perfects all !   That was the very counsel
My heart had longed to give you, and already
Had it been prompted by your own good spirit.

NATHAN.

Only must not the very first who comes
Expect to tear her from me !

LAY-BROTHER.

Surely not !

NATHAN.

Who has no greater right to her than I,
Must prove at least an earlier—

LAY-BROTHER.

Surely, surely !

NATHAN.

Which nature and the ties of blood confer.

LAY-BROTHER.

That I acknowledge.

NATHAN.

Name me then the man
Who bears relationship to her as brother,
Or uncle, cousin—any kith or kin :
To him I'll not refuse her—her so formed
By nature and by training to become
The jewel of every house, of every faith.—
You know your master and his lineage
More fully than myself, I hope.

LAY-BROTHER.

But little.

15*

I served the Knight, as you already know,
Too short a time.

NATHAN.

The mother's family,
Know you not that at least?   Was she a Stauffen?

LAY-BROTHER.

'Tis possible.   Methinks she was.

NATHAN.

Her brother,
Was he not Conrad? was he not a Templar?

LAY-BROTHER.

If I mistake not.   Stay ; I have a book
That was the Knight's.   I took it from his breast
The day we buried him at Askalon.

NATHAN.

Well ?

LAY-BROTHER.

There are prayers in it—a breviary,
We call it.   That, thought I, a Christian man
May still find useful.   Not myself indeed ;
I cannot read—

NATHAN.

No matter !   To the point !

LAY-BROTHER.

I have been told that in this little book,

At the beginning and the end, stand written
The names of both their families, inscribed
With his own hand.

NATHAN.

The very thing we want!
Run, fetch me quick this book! Its weight in gold
I'll give you, and a thousand thanks besides.
Run!

LAY-BROTHER.

Willingly; but 'tis in Arabic
The Knight has written.

NATHAN.

No matter; let me have it!
God! if I might the maiden still retain,
And let her purchase for me such a son!—
Scarce possible!—Well, come what will of it!—
But who betrayed it to the Patriarch?
I'll not forget to ask.—If it were Daja!

SCENE VIII.

DAJA *and* NATHAN.

DAJA (*hurried and embarrassed*).
Think, Nathan!

NATHAN.

Well?

DAJA.

How terrified she was,
Poor child ! There came just now a message from—

NATHAN.

The Patriarch ?

DAJA.

From the Sultan's sister, Sittah.

NATHAN.

And not the Patriarch ?

DAJA.

Sittah !   Hear you not ?
The princess Sittah sends for her.

NATHAN.

Whom ?   Recha ?
The princess send for her ?   If it be Sittah,
And not the Patriarch, sends—

DAJA.

Why think of him ?

NATHAN.

Have you heard naught from him of late ?   Quite
sure ?
And naught betrayed to him ?

DAJA.

I, him ?

NATHAN.

But say,

Where stand the messengers?

DAJA.

Before the house.

NATHAN.

'Twere best confer with them in person.   Come!
If but the Patriarch have no hand in this!   · [*Goes.*

DAJA.

And I—I tremble with another fear.
The fancied only daughter of a Jew
So rich as he, might tempt a Mussulman.
'Tis over with the Templar—he will lose her,
If I accomplish not the second step,
And tell the girl her story.—Courage—courage!
I'll seize the earliest moment we're alone—
The coming one, if I go with her there.
A little hint of it upon the way
Can do no harm.—On! Now or never! Courage!
[*Follows him.*

ACT FIFTH.

Scene I.

A room in Saladin's palace, where the money-bags are
still lying.

Saladin ; *soon after, various* Mamelukes.

Saladin (*as he enters*).

The gold still there ! and none can find the dervise !
He's stumbled on some chess-board and forgot
Himself : why not me also !—Patience !—Well ?

A Mameluke.

The longed-for tidings, Sultan !   Sultan, joy !
The caravan approaches from Kahira
With seven years' tribute from the fruitful Nile.

Saladin.

Good, Ibrahim ; you're a welcome messenger.—
At last, at last !—My thanks for your good news !

Mameluke (*waiting*).

(Out with them, then !)

Saladin.

Why wait you ?   You may go.

MAMELUKE.

Naught else then for the welcome messenger?

SALADIN.

What would you else?

MAMELUKE.

No present for the bearer?—
I'm then the first whom Saladin has learned
To pay with words. What honor! I the first
He haggles with!

SALADIN.

Take one of yonder bags.

MAMELUKE.

Not now; not though you offered me the whole.

SALADIN.

Defiant! Come, these two are yours.—In earnest?
He goes? is more magnanimous than I?
For to refuse must harder be for him
Than 'tis for me to give.—Here, Ibrahim!—
What has come o'er me that so near my end
Would make me seem another than myself?
Will Saladin not die as Saladin?
Then Saladin he ought not to have lived.

SECOND MAMELUKE.

. News, Sultan!

SALADIN.

If you come to tell—

SECOND MAMELUKE.

The transport
From Egypt has arrived.

SALADIN.

I've heard already.

SECOND MAMELUKE.

Then I am come too late.

SALADIN.

Wherefore too late?
Bear off a sack or two for your good-will.

SECOND MAMELUKE.

Makes three !

SALADIN.

If you can count as much.—Go, take them !

SECOND MAMELUKE.

There's still a third to come—if come he can.

SALADIN.

How so?

SECOND MAMELUKE.

I know not but his neck is broken.
Soon as we knew the caravan was come,
Each started off full speed. The foremost fell.

I got the start and kept it to the city,
Where Ibrahim had more knowledge of the streets.

SALADIN.

But he who fell, my friend ! The man who fell !
Ride back to meet him !

SECOND MAMELUKE.

That indeed will I !
If he's alive, half of these bags is his. [*Goes.*

SALADIN.

Another noble fellow ! Who besides
Can boast such Mamelukes ? May I not think
'Twas my example helped to fashion them ?
Away then with the thought that at the last
They should grow used to any other !

THIRD MAMELUKE.

Sultan,—

SALADIN.

Was't you who fell ?

THIRD MAMELUKE.

No. I but come to announce
That Emir Mansor, leader of the transport,
Is now dismounting.

SALADIN.

Bring him hither—quick !
Ah, here he is !

Scene II.

Emir Mansor *and* Saladin.

Saladin.

　　　　　You're welcome, Emir, welcome!
How has all gone with you?—O Mansor, Mansor,
You kept us waiting long.

Mansor.

　　　　　　　This letter tells
What tumult in Thebais your Abulkassem
Was forced to quell, ere it was safe to start.
I made all possible dispatch in coming.

Saladin.

I will believe you.—Take at once, good Mansor—
And gladly will you not?—another escort;
For you must on at once to Lebanon,
With more than half this treasure to my father.

Mansor.

Right willingly!

Saladin.

　　　　　　Make not your guard too weak.
Things are no longer safe on Lebanon.
Have you not heard?—the Templars are astir.
Be on your guard!—But come, where halts the
　　　transport?
I'll see and urge it forward.—Then to Sittah!

Scene III.

The palms before Nathan's house.

The Templar (*walking to and fro*).

I will not enter.—He'll appear at last.—
How quick, how eager to observe me once !
The time may come when e'en my frequent presence
Before his house he will forbid.—Hm—hm !
But I am most unreasonable too.—
Why so enraged against him ? As he said,
He yet has naught refused ; and Saladin
Has promised to persuade him.—Does the Christian
Hold me in closer bonds than him the Jew ?—
Who knows himself ? Why should I else begrudge
This little theft, that with abundant pains
He wrested from the Christians ?   Little theft ?
A creature such as she !   A creature !—whose ?
Not of the slave who set the block adrift
On life's waste shore, and there deserted it.
Nay, rather of the artist who conceived
In the rejected block the godlike form,
And brought it into life.—Recha's true father
Must be, despite the Christian who begot her,
Must be in all eternity the Jew.—
If I conceive her as a Christian maiden,
Deprived of all that only such a Jew

Could give—say, heart—what were her charm for
   you?
But little, nothing!—e'en her smile were naught
But gentle soft contraction of the muscles;
And that which prompts it would be undeserving
Of all the grace it wears upon her lips.
No, no—not e'en her smile! As fair or fairer
I've seen bestowed upon conceit and folly,
On mocking jests, and flatterers and gallants.
Did such enchant me or inspire the wish
To flutter out my life within its beams?
I was unconscious of it; yet am angry
With him by whom alone this higher charm
Was given.—Deserved I then the irony
Of Saladin at parting? Shame enough
That Saladin should think so! Oh, how small,
Contemptible I must have seemed to him!
All for a girl!—Curd! Curd! This will not do!
Come to yourself!—If 'twere but Daja's gossip;
Naught after all that she could prove?—But see!
He comes at last, engrossed in talk. With whom?
My friend the Brother! Then he knows it all;
Has been discovered to the Patriarch!
What has my madness done? Oh that one spark
Of passion should consume our reason thus!
Decide at once what next!—I'll stand aside,
And watch if they may not part company.

Scene IV.

Nathan *and the* Lay-brother.

Nathan.

Thanks once again, good Brother!

Lay-brother.

Mine to you.

Nathan.

Your thanks to me? for what? My obstinacy
In pressing on you what you do not want?
If yours had yielded—good; but you were firm—
You would not be a richer man than I.

Lay-brother.

Besides, the book's not mine; it is the daughter's—
The daughter's sole paternal heritage.—
She has yourself indeed. God grant that ne'er
You may repent your goodness to her!

Nathan.

Never;
That can I never! Fear not!

Lay-brother.

Nay, but then—
The Patriarchs and the Templars—

16*

NATHAN.

Can inflict
No evil that shall make me aught regret—
That least of all !—But are you well assured
A Templar set your Patriarch on the scent ?

LAY-BROTHER.

It must be ; for a Templar just before
Had speech with him, and what I heard so sounded.

NATHAN.

There is but one in all Jerusalem,
And him I know : he is my friend ; a man,
Young, noble, frank.

LAY-BROTHER.

Right ; 'tis the very same.
A difference lies between what one must seem
Before the world, and what one is.

NATHAN.

Too true.—
Whoe'er he be, I dare his worst or best !
Your book, good brother, bids me all defy.
I go with it straightway to Saladin.

LAY-BROTHER.

Good luck to you !   Here will I leave you then.

NATHAN.

Without a sight of her ?   Come soon again,
And often.—If the Patriarch but to-day

Might not be told !—Yet wherefore? Nay; this day
Disclose whate'er you will.

LAY-BROTHER.

Not I. Farewell! [*Goes*

NATHAN.

Forget us not, good Brother !—Gracious God !
Why can I not fall down upon my knees
Beneath this open heaven ! How has this knot,
So long my secret terror, come unloosed
As of itself! How light my heart has grown
To think there's nothing further in the world
I need to hide ; that I can walk erect
Before my fellow-men as in Thy sight,
O Thou, who needest not to judge of man
According to his deeds—so seldom his !

———

SCENE V.

NATHAN *and the* TEMPLAR.

TEMPLAR.

Wait; take me with you, Nathan ; wait !

NATHAN.

Who calls?
You, Knight? Where were you that I met you not
Before the Sultan ?

TEMPLAR.

We but missed each other.

Take it not ill !

NATHAN.

Not I ! but Saladin—

TEMPLAR.

You just had left him when—

NATHAN.

You spoke with him ?

Then all is well.

TEMPLAR.

But he would speak with both.

NATHAN.

So much the better.   Come !   I'm on my way.

TEMPLAR.

May I inquire who quitted you but now ?

NATHAN.

You surely do not know him ?

TEMPLAR.

Was it not

That honest Brother who is oft employed
To scent the Patriarch's game ?

NATHAN.

May be the same ;

He's with the Patriarch.

TEMPLAR.

Not a bad device /
To make simplicity the villain's scout. /

NATHAN.

It must be dull simplicity—not honest.

TEMPLAR.

No Patriarch would acknowledge any honest.

NATHAN.

I'd vouch for him.   The man would ne'er assist
His Patriarch in aught evil.

TEMPLAR.

So at least
He'd have us think.—But said he naught of me?

NATHAN.

He named you not—knows not your name, perhaps.

TEMPLAR.

No ; hardly.

NATHAN.

Of a Templar said he something—

TEMPLAR.

What?

NATHAN.

That which clearly proved he meant not you.

TEMPLAR.

Who knows? Let's hear.

NATHAN.

That one of you accused me
Before the Patriarch—

TEMPLAR.

One accused you? No;
There, with his leave, he lied. Believe me, Nathan!
I'm not a man who would disown his deeds.
What I have done, I've done. Nor am I one
Who would defend his every deed as right.
Why blush to own a fault when I'm resolved
I will redeem it? Know I not what power
Lies in such resolution?—Hear me, Nathan!
I am the Brother's Templar who, he says,
Accused you to the Patriarch. Well you know
The provocation which had made my blood
Rush boiling through my veins. Fool!—I had come
With all my heart and soul to throw myself
Into your arms. How coldly you received me;
With what indifference—an indifference worse
Than coldness; how you labored studiously
To evade me; with what far-fetched questionings
You wished to make it seem you gave me answer;—
These things I must not dare to think of yet,
If I would keep my temper.—Hear me, Nathan!—
In this excitement, Daja stole upon me,

And flung her secret in my face.   The key
It seemed to all your strange demeanor.

NATHAN.

How?

TEMPLAR.

Nay, hear me out !—I fancied you unwilling
To give again into a Christian hand
What from the Christians you had stolen, and thought
To settle it for good and all by putting
The knife to your throat.

NATHAN.

For good and all? for good?
I see no good about it.

TEMPLAR.

Hear me, Nathan !
I did not well.   May be, you are not guilty.
That foolish Daja knows not what she says.
She likes you not ; hoped thus to injure you,
May be—may be !   I am a simpleton—
Forever in extremes ;—now much too hot,
And now as much too cold.   That grant I too !
Forgive me, Nathan !

NATHAN.

If you take me so—

TEMPLAR.

In short—I did seek out the Patriarch,

But named you not.   That, as I said, was false.
I only set before him such a case
To learn his judgment.   That I might have spared.
Knew I him not already for a knave?
Why not have called you to account myself?
Wherefore, poor girl, expose her to the risk
Of losing such a father?—What befell?
The Patriarch's baseness, faithful to itself,
Restored me to my senses.—Hear me, Nathan—
Hear to the end!   Suppose he knew your name—
What then?   He has no right to take the girl
If she belong to any but yourself.
From your home only can he have the right
To drag her to the cloister.—Therefore give—
Give her to me, and let him come.   Aha!
Let him beware how he shall take my wife!
Give her me—quick!—be she your child or not!
A Christian, Jewess, neither—naught care I!
I'll put no questions to you—neither now
Nor ever in my life.   Be as it may!

NATHAN.

Deem you it necessary for me then
To hide the truth?   ˋ

TEMPLAR.

Be as it may!

NATHAN.

I ne'er
To you or any who had claim to know

Denied she was a Christian, and to me
But an adopted daughter.   Why, you say,
Conceal it from herself?   To her alone
Need I excuse myself.

TEMPLAR.

Not e'en to her !
Let her ne'er look on you with other eyes.
Oh, spare her the disclosure !   You alone
Have still disposal of her.   Give her me !
I pray you, Nathan, give her me !   I only
Again can save her to you, and I will.

NATHAN.

Could—could !   No longer possible—too late !

TEMPLAR.

How so—too late ?

NATHAN.

Thanks to the Patriarch—

TEMPLAR.

Thanks to the Patriarch !   Wherefore thanks to
   him ?
Has he desired to earn our thanks ?   For what ?

NATHAN.

That we have learned her family ; have learned
Into whose hands she may be given up.

TEMPLAR.

The thanks I leave to those he has obliged.

17

NATHAN.

From theirs must you receive her now, not mine.

TEMPLAR.

Poor Recha, how must all this fall on you !
What were a happiness to other orphans
Is your misfortune.—Nathan !—Where are they,
These relatives ?

NATHAN.

Where are they ?

TEMPLAR.

Who are they ?

NATHAN.

A brother first ; from him she must be sought.

TEMPLAR.

A brother !   And this brother, what is he ?
Priest—soldier ?   Let me hear what hope I have.

NATHAN.

Neither—or both.   I've not yet learned him quite.

TEMPLAR.

What more ?

NATHAN.

An honest man ; to whom our Recha
May well be trusted.

TEMPLAR.

Yet a Christian !—Nathan,

How can I understand you?—Be not angry!—
Must she not play the Christian with the Christians,
And take at last the character she plays?
Will not the grain you sowed so pure, be choked
By weeds at last? And you so careless of it!
This notwithstanding can you say—you say—
She may be safely trusted with her brother?

NATHAN.

I think it—hope it. Should she want for aught
With him, has she not still yourself and me?

TEMPLAR.

Can any thing be wanting her with him?
Will not dear brother give his little sister
Enough of food and clothing, finery
And dainties? What can little sister want
Besides?—A husband, to be sure! Well, well;
That too, in time, dear brother will provide;
The best that can be had! and all the better
The more he is a Christian.—Nathan, Nathan!
Why fashion such an angel to be marred
By other men?

NATHAN.

Fear not; she will remain
Abundantly deserving of our love.

TEMPLAR.

Nay, say not that; of my love say it not!
My love will brook no change in her—not one;

No veriest trifle—e'en a name.—But hold !
Has a suspicion reached her of her fate?

NATHAN.

Perhaps ; yet hardly could I tell from whom.

TEMPLAR.

It matters not ;—I must, I will be first
To let her know the fate that threatens her.
My purpose ne'er to see, ne'er speak with her
Till I might call her mine, is changed.   I haste—

NATHAN.

Stay ; whither would you go ?

TEMPLAR.

              To her ; to her,
To learn if in her maiden soul there lie
Enough of manhood for the one resolve
Which only would be worthy of her.

NATHAN.

              What ?

TEMPLAR.

To let her heart no longer dwell on you
Or on her brother—

NATHAN.

But ?—

TEMPLAR.

              To follow me ;
Though 'twere to make herself a Moslem's wife.

NATHAN.

Stay; you would find her not. She is with Sittah,
The Sultan's sister.

TEMPLAR.

When was that—and why?

NATHAN.

If you would see the brother with them—come!

TEMPLAR.

Whose brother? Sittah's—Recha's?

NATHAN.

Both, perhaps.
But come with me—I pray you, come with me!

[Leads him away.

———

SCENE VI.

Sittah's harem. SITTAH *and* RECHA *in conversation.*

SITTAH.

How I rejoice to see you, darling child!
But be not so reserved, so shy, so troubled;—
Be gay—more talkative—more friendly with me.

RECHA.

Princess—

SITTAH.

No, no; not Princess: call me Sittah—
Your friend—your sister—mother, if you will!

17*

That might I almost be.—So young, so wise,
So good ; with so much knowledge !—Ah, how much
You must have read !

RECHA.

I must have read !—Ah, Sittah,
You're laughing at your foolish little sister.
I scarce know how to read.

SITTAH.

What? story-teller !
You scarce know how?

RECHA.

My father's hand a little.
I thought you spoke of books.

SITTAH.

Yes, yes—of books

RECHA.

No ; I should find it hard to read in books.

SITTAH.

Are you in earnest?

RECHA.

I am quite in earnest.
My father cares not for that cold book-learning
That's printed on the brain by lifeless signs.

SITTAH.

What do you tell me !—Yet he's partly right.
Then all you know—

RECHA.

Is only from his lips.
Scarce anything, but I could tell you how,
And where, and why, my father taught it me.

SITTAH.

Thus all is better woven into one :
The whole soul learns at once.

RECHA.

And Sittah too—
Has surely little read, or nothing.

SITTAH.

Why ?
I would not boast the contrary ; but why ?
Your reason ; tell me candidly—your reason ?

RECHA.

She is so true and honest ; so unspoiled ;
Acts out herself so naturally ;—

SITTAH.

Well ?

RECHA.

My father says books rarely leave us so.

SITTAH.

How wise a man he is !

RECHA.

Yes ; is he not ?

SITTAH.

How near he hits the mark!

RECHA.

Ah, does he not?

And yet this father—

SITTAH.

What disturbs you, love?

RECHA.

This father—

SITTAH.

Heavens! You weep?

RECHA.

This father—Ah,
I must speak out;—my heart must have relief!
    [*Throws herself, overpowered by her tears, at
    Sittah's feet.*

SITTAH.

Recha! What ails you, child?

RECHA.

This father—must—
Ah, must I lose!

SITTAH.

Must lose your father! Why?
Compose yourself!—Impossible!—Stand up!

RECHA.

It shall not be in vain that you have offered
To be my friend, my sister!

SITTAH.

I am both.

But rise ; else must I call for help.

RECHA (*controls herself, and rises*).

Forgive ;
Your pardon !—In my grief I had forgot
To whom I spoke.   No moaning, no despair
Avails with Sittah.   Naught has power with her
But cold, calm reason.   Whosesoever cause
That pleads before her, conquers.

SITTAH.

Well ?

RECHA.

My friend,
My sister, suffer not—oh, suffer not
Another father to be forced upon me !

SITTAH.

Another father forced upon you, love ?
Who has the power, the wish to do it ?

RECHA.

Who ?
My good, bad Daja has the wish, and claims
The power.   Know you her not, this good, bad Daja ?
God pardon her for it—reward her for it !
Such good as she has done me—and such harm !

SITTAH.

Done harm to you !   Small good is in her then.

RECHA.

Nay, much—how much !

SITTAH.

Who is she?

RECHA.

She's a Christian,
Who tended me in childhood with such care ;
You cannot think !   She scarcely let me miss
My mother.—God reward her !—But besides,
She so distressed and tortured me !

SITTAH.

With what?'
And wherefore?

RECHA.

Ah, poor woman !   As I said,
She is a Christian, and from very love
Must torture me.   She is of those fanatics
Who think they know the universal, true,
And only road to God.

SITTAH.

I understand.

RECHA.

And feel a charge upon them to conduct
The feet of every wanderer thitherward.
They scarce can otherwise.   If it be true

This is the only road that leads aright,
Can they resign themselves to see their friends
Advancing on another which descends
To death, eternal death? They needs must love
And hate one at the selfsame time.—Not that
Has forced from me such loud complaints
Against her. Gladly would I still have borne
Her sighs and prayers, her threats and warnings—
    gladly!
For good and useful were the thoughts they roused.
Besides, how not be flattered too at heart
At being held so precious and so dear
By any, that the thought of losing us
For all eternity cannot be borne?

SITTAH.

'Tis true.

RECHA.

       But this—this is too much! 'Gainst this
I've no defence; not patience, not reflection,
Not anything!

SITTAH.

What? Whom?

RECHA.

             What she but now
Pretended to reveal.

SITTAH.

Reveal but now?

RECHA.

But now.—Upon our way to you we neared
A ruined Christian temple.   Suddenly
She stopped ; appeared to struggle with herself ;
Directed now to heaven and now on me
Her streaming eyes.   ''Come,'' finally she said,
''We'll take the shortest path through yonder
      temple.''
She went ; I followed, gazing with affright
Upon the tottering ruins.   Once again
She stopped ; and I beheld myself with her
Before the steps of a decaying altar.
Ah, how I felt, when here, with burning tears
And wringing of her hands, she threw herself
Upon the ground before me !—

SITTAH.

              Darling child !

RECHA.

And by the Deity who there had heard
So many prayers, and worked so many wonders,
Conjured me—yes, with looks of true compassion—
Conjured me to have pity on myself !—
At least to pardon her, for she must tell
Her Church's claim upon me.

SITTAH.

             Ah, poor girl ;
'Tis as I thought.

RECHA.

I had been born, she said,
Of Christian parents ; I had been baptized ;
I was not Nathan's child—he not my father !
God ! God ! He not my father !—Sittah ! Sittah !
Here at your feet again behold me—

SITTAH.

Recha !
I pray you, rise ! My brother comes ! Stand up !

———

SCENE VII.

SALADIN *and the preceding.*

SALADIN.

What trouble, Sittah ?

SITTAH.

· She's beside herself !

SALADIN.

Who is it ?

SITTAH.

You remember—

SALADIN.

Nathan's daughter !
What ails her ?

18

SITTAH.

Child, control yourself!—The Sultan—

RECHA (*her head bowed to the ground, drags herself*
upon her knees to Saladin's feet).

I rise not; look not on the Sultan's face;
Behold not on his brow and in his eyes
The bright reflection of eternal love
And justice, till—

SITTAH.

Rise; rise!

RECHA.

He promise me—

SALADIN.

I promise;—be it what it may!

RECHA.

No more
Nor less than this—to leave to me my father,
And me to him.   I know not who besides
Would be my father; who can want to be.
I will not know.—But is it only blood
That makes the father—only blood?

SALADIN (*raising her*).

I see.
Who was so heartless as to name the thing
To you?   Is it already settled—proved?

RECHA.

It must be ;—Daja says 'twas from my nurse
She learned it.

SALADIN.

From your nurse?

RECHA.

Who felt constrained
Upon her death-bed to confess it to her.

SALADIN.

Upon her death-bed? Possibly she wandered.—
But were it true—you're right! The blood alone
Makes not the father—scarce a wild beast's father.
At most, it but confers the earliest right
To earn the name. Fear not ;—hark to my counsel!
When these two fathers come to quarrel for you,
Dismiss them both and take the third ;—take me
To be your father!

SITTAH.

Yes, dear Recha, yes!

SALADIN.

I'd make a right good father.—Hold ;—still better!
What need of fathers? What if they should die?
But seek betimes for one who would brave all
To live for you. Has none such yet been found?

SITTAH.

Make her not blush!

SALADIN.

The very thing I wished !
If blushes make the ugly fair, they surely
Will make the fair still fairer.—I have bid
Your father, Nathan, hither, and another—
Another with him.   Guess you not his name?
Hither—with your permission, Sittah.

SITTAH.
                              Brother !

SALADIN.

Call up a rosy blush for him, dear child.

RECHA.

A blush—for whom ?

SALADIN.

Ah, little hypocrite !
Grow pale then, if you choose ;—just as you will
And can.
          [*A female slave enters and addresses Sittah.*
Are they arrived already?

SITTAH.
                              Good ;
You may admit them.—It is they, dear brother !

LAST SCENE.

NATHAN *and the* TEMPLAR, *with the preceding.*

SALADIN.

Welcome, my dear, good friends!—You, Nathan, you
Must I address the first. Send you and fetch
Your money back whene'er you want it.

NATHAN.
                                   Sultan—

SALADIN.

'Tis now my turn to be of service;—

NATHAN.
                                   Sultan—

SALADIN.

The caravan is come. I'm rich again
As I've not been for many a day. Come, come;
Say what you need to start some enterprise
Of magnitude. You tradesmen, like ourselves,
Can scarce have too much money.

NATHAN.
                          Why begin
With such a trifle?—There are weeping eyes
That I am more concerned with drying.—Recha!
                          [*Approaches her.*
You have been weeping;—what distresses you?
Are you not still my daughter?
                     18*

RECHA.

O my father !

NATHAN.

We understand each other.   'Tis enough !—
Be cheerful ; be collected.—Let your heart
Be still your own : let but no other loss
Have threatened that—your father is not lost !

RECHA.

No other ; none.

TEMPLAR.

None !   Then I was deceived.
What we fear not to lose, we never thought
Nor wished to own.—So be it.—That changes all.
We came here, Saladin, at your command.
But I misled you ;—take no further trouble.

SALADIN.

Hasty again, young man !   Must everything
Consult your pleasure then—all guess your thoughts ?

TEMPLAR.

But, Sultan—hear you, see you not yourself ?

SALADIN.

I do indeed ;—pity you made not sure
Of your position.

TEMPLAR.

'Tis no longer doubtful.

SALADIN.

Who thus presumes upon a benefit,
Revokes it. What you saved is not your own
Because you saved it. Else as good a hero
Were any thief whose greed will brave the fire.

[*Approaches Recha to lead her to the Templar.*
Come, darling, come ; be not too strict with him.
Were he aught else, were he less hot and proud,
He might not have preserved you. Let the one
Excuse the other.—Come ; put him to shame ;
Do that which should be his—confess your love—
Give him your hand ; and if he should disdain you—
Should he forget how infinitely more
You did for him by this than he for you—
What did he then for you ? get singed a little !
But what was that ?—then has he naught of Assad,
Naught of my brother ; wears his likeness only,
And not his heart.—Come, love !

SITTAH.

Yes ; go, love, go !
Your gratitude would deem that little—nothing.

NATHAN.

Hold, Saladin ! hold, Sittah !

SALADIN.

What—you also ?

NATHAN.

There is another has a right to speak.

SALADIN.

Who doubts it?   Such a foster-father, Nathan,
Unquestionably has a voice—the first,
If you desire.   You see I know the whole.

NATHAN.

Not quite the whole.—I speak not of myself.
There is another, quite another, Sultan,
Whom also I entreat you first to hear.

SALADIN.

Who—who?

NATHAN.

Her brother.

SALADIN.

Recha's brother?

NATHAN.

Yes.

RECHA.

My brother !   Have I then a brother?

TEMPLAR (*rousing himself from his brooding*).

Where ?
Where is this brother?   Not yet here ?   'Twas here
I was to meet him.

NATHAN.

Patience !

TEMPLAR (*with bitterness*).

He's imposed
A father on her—why not find a brother?

SALADIN.

That also! Christian! such a base suspicion
Would ne'er have come from Assad's lips.—Good!
   good!
Keep on!

NATHAN.

Forgive him! I forgive him gladly.
Should we do better, circumstanced like him,
And young?   [*Approaching the Templar kindly.*
   Quite natural that want of trust
Should breed suspicion, Knight. Had you confessed
Your rightful name at once—

TEMPLAR.

How?

NATHAN.

You're no Stauffen.

TEMPLAR.

Who am I then?

NATHAN.

Your name's not Curd von Stauffen.

TEMPLAR.

What then?

NATHAN.

Tis Leu von Filneck.

TEMPLAR.

How?

NATHAN.

You start !

TEMPLAR.

With reason.   Who asserts it ?

NATHAN.

I ; and more
Have I to tell you.   Yet I charge you not
With falsehood.

TEMPLAR.

No ?

NATHAN.

That name may be your own
With equal right.

TEMPLAR.

I think so !   (Well for him
He said it.)

NATHAN.

For your mother was a Stauffen
Her brother, to whose charge in Germany
You were committed when the ungenial air
Had forced your parents to the East again,

Was Curd von Stauffen, who adopted you
Perhaps in place of children of his own.
How long since you came hither? Lives he still?

TEMPLAR.

What shall I answer?—All is as you say;
But he himself is dead. I came not hither
Until the last detachment of our Order—
But—but—how bears all this on Recha's brother?

NATHAN.

Your father—

TEMPLAR.

How? Him too—you knew him too?

NATHAN.

He was my friend.

TEMPLAR.

Your friend! How possible?

NATHAN.

The name of Wolf von Filneck did he bear;
But was no German—

TEMPLAR.

Know you also that?

NATHAN.

Was wedded to a German, and had followed
Your mother into Germany awhile.

TEMPLAR.

No more, I pray !—But Recha's brother, Nathan—
Her brother?

NATHAN.

Is yourself.

TEMPLAR.

I—I her brother !

RECHA.

Ah, he my brother !

SALADIN.

They are brother and sister !

SITTAH.

They brother and sister !

RECHA (*advancing to him*).

Ah, my brother !

TEMPLAR (*drawing back*).

Brother !

RECHA (*checking herself, and turning to Nathan*).

It cannot—cannot be !   There's no response
Within his heart.—We are impostors !   God !

SALADIN (*to the Templar*).

Impostors !   Do you think it—can you think it?
Yourself the impostor?   All in you is false ;
Face, voice, and bearing—nothing yours.   Refuse
To acknowledge such a sister?   Go—begone !

TEMPLAR (*approaching him humbly*).
Mistake not you too, Sultan, my surprise.
Ne'er saw you Assad at a time like this.
Oh, be not thus unjust to him and me !
[Hurrying to Nathan.
You give me, Nathan, and you take away—
With full hands both.—But no ; you give me more,
More infinitely than you take away.
[Embracing Recha.
My sister, O my sister !

NATHAN.
Henceforth Blanda
Von Filneck.

TEMPLAR.
Blanda—Blanda—no more Recha—
Your Recha then no more ? God !—You reject
  her—
You give her back her Christian name—reject her
Because of me ! Oh, wherefore call on her
To make atonement, Nathan ?

NATHAN.
What atonement ?—
My children, O my children ! For will he,
The brother of my daughter, not become
Another child to me ?
*[While Nathan gives himself up to their caresses,
    Saladin, surprised and uneasy, turns to Sittah.*

19

SALADIN.

What say you, Sittah?

SITTAH.

I'm deeply moved.

SALADIN.

And I—I feel my heart
Recoil before a feeling deeper still.
Prepare yourself as best you may!

SITTAH.

For what?

SALADIN (*to Nathan*).

A word with you—a word!
  [*As Nathan joins the Sultan, Sittah approaches
  the brother and sister to express her sympathy;
  Nathan and Saladin speak in whispers.*

Hark to me, Nathan;—
Did you not say—

NATHAN.

What?

SALADIN.

That from Germany
Their father came not—was no German born?
What was he then—whence came he?

NATHAN.

That he ne'er

Confided to me.   Naught of it I learned
From his own lips.

SALADIN.

And was he then no Frank—
No native of the West?

NATHAN.

That he confessed.
He spoke most readily in Persian.

SALADIN.

Persian !
What need I more ?   It is—it was himself !

NATHAN.

Who ?

SALADIN.

'Twas my brother, surely—'twas my Assad !

NATHAN.

Since you yourself have guessed it, read in this
Its confirmation.   [*Handing him the breviary.*

SALADIN (*opening it eagerly*).

Ah, his hand—that too
I recognize again !

NATHAN.

They know of naught.
It rests with you alone to say how much
They e'er shall know.

SALADIN (*turning over the leaves*).

And shall I not acknowledge
My brother's children — my own blood — my children—
Not own them?   Shall I give them up to you?
(*Aloud.*)
'Tis they—'tis they, dear Sittah—it is they!
My brother's and your brother's children—both!
[*He hastens to embrace them.*

SITTAH (*following*).

What do I hear?—It must, it must be so!

SALADIN (*to the Templar*).

You must—must love me now, hot-headed boy!
(*To Recha.*)
Now am I really what I asked to be—
Like it or not!

SITTAH.

I too—I too!

SALADIN (*again to the Templar*).

My son—
My Assad—Assad's son!

TEMPLAR.

I of your blood!
Then were those dreams that clustered round my childhood
Not merely empty dreams. [*Falls at the Sultan's feet.*

SALADIN *(raising him).*

Behold the knave !
He something knew of this, and yet could wish
To make me be his murderer.   Ah, the knave !

[*They embrace.*

(*The curtain falls.*)
19*

ESSAY ON

NATHAN THE WISE.

[Condensed.]

NATHAN THE WISE is universally acknowledged to
be among the most important poems in German
literature, yet hardly any other great poem has
as many enemies. Some critics think lightly
of it as a work of art—a drama ; others, by far the
greater number, oppose it on account of the religious tone which they think underlies it. Both
opinions have their leaders, and the leaders their
chorus, which echoes the sentence and gives it circulation. Thus it has come to pass that this poem
is besieged by an army of prejudices, which most
persons accept before they are in condition to examine the subject for themselves. The wisest course,
under such circumstances, is to let the judgment of
others affect us as little as possible, and to give ourselves up unreservedly to the influence of the work
itself. Let us then proceed to consider, not so much
the judgments passed upon Nathan, as the poem itself.

GENESIS OF THE POEM.

About the year 1770, there simultaneously appeared in Germany an unusual number of great works. Besides Lessing's *Emilia Galotti*, there appeared Goethe's first productions, *Werther* and *Götz*. Lessing was himself in the prime of his manhood, at the height of his art, from which he never declined, but in the fulness of time was to be snatched away. After the *Emilia Galotti* he appears to have abandoned the field of poetry. His office in Wolfenbüttel, the journey to Italy, the publication of the *Wolfenbüttel Fragments*, and the controversies connected with it, kept his interests and powers busy in other directions. Whoever is called to be a reformer must accept the duties of a soldier. These duties Lessing fulfilled with such great ability and success that Goethe and Schiller could speak of him in one of their *Xenien* as the Achilles of German literature.

Lessing's poetical works stand in very close connection with his critical. The *Literaturbriefe* are followed by *Minna von Barnhelm*, the *Dramaturgie* by *Emilia Galotti*, and the *Antigötze* by *Nathan the Wise*. The connection in all three cases is evident. But in the last we should greatly err in attributing the origin of the *Nathan* entirely to the *Antigötze*, as if it were only a continuation of that controversy. The idea of our poem dates further back. Between the years 1774 and 1778 Lessing had published some fragments of a work left by the Hamburg Professor, Hermann Samuel Reimarus, as if they had been found among the manuscript treasures of the Wolfenbüttel library. He purposely, and by promise,

.

concealed the name of the author. The published extracts were therefore called the Wolfenbüttel Fragments, and the unknown author, the Wolfenbüttel Fragmentist. The work of Reimarus was, as it professed to be, a defence of the religion of reason by a refutation of that of revelation. It was an attack upon the biblical religion of both Testaments, founded on a criticism of the Canon. The Fragments, especially the last, upon the history and person of Jesus, kindled the controversy which especially Melchior Götze, a Lutheran preacher in Hamburg, began and carried on with most violent zeal. He aimed less at refuting the fragments (which Lessing would have liked, as he was by no means in sympathy with their spirit), than at convicting of heresy, and dooming to damnation both author and editor. In the eyes of the Hamburg pastor the Fragments were destructive of religion, and therefore dangerous to the State, because subversive of belief in the Bible. He accused the editor of having made himself a participator in the crime, asserting that his answers to the unknown author were only for appearance' sake, and made the case worse rather than better.

Lessing's reply, at once a defence and a refutation, are his famous letters against Götze, the *Antigötze.* They are specimens of controversial writing, unique in the domain of theological literature, from the bearing and importance of the question, the extent of ground covered, and the personal ability—unsurpassed by any man of his time—which Lessing brought to bear. His object was not only to defend the Protestants' right to freedom of inquiry against the Lutheran zeal for belief in the letter, but also to maintain the independence of every religion, espe•

cially the Christian, of all adherence to the letter.
His argument was, that as religion is older than
Scripture, Christianity older than the Bible, it must
have existed before the Canon, and cannot therefore
be made to depend on the letter of the Canon. The
object was to search for the archetype of religion in
the right place, in order to see its written image in
the right light.   Hence arose a multitude of questions about the origin of the Canon, the spirit of
primitive Christianity, and the essence of religion.
The controversy between Lessing and Götze was cut
short.   As early as 1778, the public authorities in-
terfered.   The Consistory of Brunswick wished the
thing suppressed, and the ministry deprived Lessing
of the privilege of printing his book, confiscated
the Fragments, and forbade the continuance of the
controversy.*

At this time of public ill-treatment, to which were
added heavy domestic sorrows, a fresh impulse was
given to the idea of Nathan, which had been begun
some years before.   The night of the tenth of Au-
gust, 1778, he resolved to finish the work.   Early in
November the full prose sketch was finished, and in
the same month the metrical framework was begun.
This enlarged the piece far beyond the limits of the
sketch, and gave shape and life to the different characters.   In March, 1779, the poem was completed
in its present form.   Thus is shown the connection
between the *Nathan* and the *Antigötze* in point of

* Reimarus' complete work, and his theological position, have
been treated in an exhaustive manner by D. Fr. Strauss, under the
title of *Hermann Samuel Reimarus and his Defence of the Rationai
Worshippers of God* (1862); and the relations of Lessing to Reimarus,
and of the *Antigötze* to *Nathan the Wise,* are similarly treated of in
a discourse by the same author, entitled *Lessing's Nathan the Wise*
(1864).

time and matter. In the controversy with Götze the question had come up, "What is the essence of Religion?" "What is the nature of the Religion which precedes belief in the letter?" In Nathan, Lessing meant to answer these questions by representing to us the true and original conditions of religion in their most living and unmistakable forms, embodied in characters to which he could point and say, "That is what I mean." The check to his controversy with Götze had changed the librarian back into the dramatist. "I must see if they will let me preach undisturbed in my own pulpit, the theatre," he said. Thus polemics helped to give to the world this "son of his advancing old age," as Lessing himself called the Nathan; but they did not create it. And all of Lessing's friends who expected from this connection of the poem with the controversy, a polemical or satirical drama, were happily disappointed.

At a time when he wrote poetry with difficulty, Lessing could hardly have finished his Nathan in a few months, if he had not conceived it long before. *Emilia Galotti* was begun fifteen years before it was completed. When Lessing told his brother of his determination to write the Nathan, he said it was a drama which he had sketched out many years before. Perhaps the design of it goes back to the first period of his literary activity. At least we find a kindred theme among the subjects occupying him then. One of those *Rettungen* which Lessing wrote at that time, treats of an Italian philosopher of the sixteenth century, Hieronymus Cardanus, famed as a mathematician, who, in his *de Subtilitate*, had compared the four religions of the world—the Heathen, Jewish, Christian, and Moslem. His work took the form of a colloquy, in which each of the speakers represented one of the four religions, and defended it against the others.   It was objected that the author had treated Christianity slightingly, and gave it the lowest place.   Lessing, in his essay, defended him from this charge.   He claimed that the opposite fault might rather be found with him— that he did not furnish the Jewish and Mahometan religions with as strong arguments as he should. He might have made out a much better case for them.   Had Lessing been pleading their cause, he would have made the Jew and the Mahometan speak very differently ; and he proceeds to sketch out a little plan of defence for them.   This idea reminds us somewhat of our poem.   The Christian, Jewish, and Mahometan religions enter the colloquial lists against one another.   Each one is to plead its own cause, and in such a way that the anti-Christian religions may have justice done them.   Why might not the thought even then have occurred to him of treating this subject dramatically ?

Yet Lessing needed for this a more personal and living subject than he could draw from Cardanus's colloquy.   He found it in Boccacio's Decameron.   The story is briefly this.   Saladin's treasury is empty.   He needs large sums of money, and knows not where to obtain them.   In this emergency he remembers that there lives in Alexandria a Jew, Melchisedek — rich and usurious.   He sends for him, and tries by a captious question to bring him into his power.   The Jew must tell the Sultan which of the three laws he considers the true one, the Jewish, Christian, or Saracen.   However he may answer, there seems no escape.   If he says the Jewish, he insults the Sultan's faith ; if he names any other, he denies his own. The Jew's decision is soon made. He answers with the story of the three rings, in nearly the same way that it is told in Nathan the Wise.

Yet there is one important difference between Lessing and Boccacio. With the latter, the ring is only a jewel, entitling the possessor to nothing but the inheritance and the position of head of the family. With Lessing, on the contrary, it bears a higher significance. "It had the secret power of giving favor, in sight of God and man, to him who wore it with a believing heart."

In Nathan, the ring has the power of winning hearts, therefore of ennobling hearts, for the latter is made the condition of the former. Only he who sows love, reaps love. He who receives the most love, because he has given the most, is undoubtedly in possession of the true ring. But all three are disputing. Each considers himself the favored one, and the others impostors. Each one hates the others. So long as this intolerant, selfish strife continues, the treasure of love is not among them ; so long the true ring remains undiscovered ; so long all three that are produced are counterfeit. And how if the true ring should declare itself? if its power should begin to work? Then one is the most beloved, and must therefore have earned love ; he must have conquered the hearts of the others. And if one is the best beloved, there must be love, and therefore purity of heart, in the others. Each one will, in proportion to his power of self-renunciation, love his neighbor, understand his views, and practise forbearance. There is a toleration which the world commends, and which most men practise, priding themselves upon it as a virtue,

20

though it is the easiest thing in the world. It requires us only to be indifferent to the beliefs of others. When we have once thrown religion upon that heap of things we characterize as "trash," it is very easy not to concern ourselves about it in other people, especially as the reasoning faculty is thereby saved a great labor. I know not whether this so-called toleration is better than its opposite. More convenient it certainly is, and just as certainly it is not genuine toleration; for real toleration bears with the beliefs and habits of others, not from indifference, but from comprehension—from knowledge of human nature—from that interest which Leibnitz well calls "the love which is identical with wisdom."

THE PLOT.

This idea determines the purpose and subject of the poem. What appears in the fable of the rings as the distant goal of the ages—the perfect reconciliation of the human race, after emerging, purified, from their sectional religions—the poem aims to anticipate and present to us, on a reduced scale, in a family circle in which worthy representatives of the three hostile religions are united after a long separation. A story had therefore to be invented which should bring about such a union of Jew, Christian, and Moslem. This story is, as Lessing expresses it, "the interesting episode which he has woven about the tale of the three rings."

Moral power is measured by the obstacles met and overcome. In times when the world is glutted with sectional hatred, and wars are waged in the name of religion, true toleration—pure love of hu-

manity, founded on unselfishness—will be best, because most severely, tested ; and in just such times
will this be manifested in certain rare characters.
The Crusades, therefore, form an appropriate theatre
for our story.   After the religious passions have un-
dergone an unusual strain, there is an inevitable reaction.   The most violent intolerance gives place to
that easy tolerance which begins to neutralize all
religious differences.   True toleration is something
different from this. The fourth Crusade gives marked
evidence that the interest in religion was diminish-
ing with the passions it engendered, and that a difference of belief had in some cases no longer a
dividing power.   A Templar goes over to Saladin ;
a Christian king knights a Mussulman—the Sultan's
cousin ; and even an alliance by marriage is planned
between Saladin and Cœur de Lion.   It is the period
when the Jewish and Moslem culture stands so high,
that their philosophers can instruct the Christian
theologians in regard to Aristotle, and influence
Christian culture in many important ways.

Especially did the Crusades represent and produce
a great crisis in the religious condition of the Christian world.   They worked upon the religious passions—inflaming, blunting, purifying them.   Their
effect stands in marked contrast to their cause.   The
Crusades sprang from a passionate yearning for a
faith ; after that yearning was satisfied, they necessarily
ended in one of those great and fruitful disenchant-
ments which enrich the world so much, and are
never bought too dearly.   The Crusaders sought,
and resolved to win, the sepulchre of Christ ; and
what they found, won, and lost again, was—a sepulchre.   They made for themselves the discovery that
the grave was empty,—and, through their experience,

the saying by the well of Samaria received a new fulfilment : " God is a spirit, and they who worship him, must worship him in spirit and in truth." We may say that this great tragedy purified the faith through the passions, and was, to use an expression of Aristotle, "A true katharsis."

The source from which he took his theme led Lessing back to the time and person of Saladin, who was ruler of Jerusalem toward the end of the twelfth century, from 1187 to 1193. The chronological contradictions, which Lessing did not attempt to avoid, prevent our assigning an exact year to the supposed events.

On the side of art, the composition has undeniable faults. What a difference, in this respect, between it and the Emilia Galotti ! In Emilia Galotti the thread of the drama is tightly drawn, the flow of incidents is smooth and natural, and the motive of every action consistently dramatic. In Nathan the separate threads are loosely and artificially joined, and the incidents are not always consistent with the characters, but often are mere episodes of one another. There is hardly anything less characteristic for the dramatic poet than the resemblance of two faces ; it can be made obvious by no manner of action or any poetical means. The author of Laocoön was perfectly aware of this. And yet he uses this motive twice in Nathan, not only incidentally, but as of effective and decisive influence. It is lucky that the Templar resembles his father so much— lucky that the Sultan recognizes this resemblance at the last moment—lucky that Nathan himself discovers the same resemblance in time. The whole story at last turns upon the features of the Templar. So superficial, in the literal sense of the term, dramatic motives must not be. This connection between the Templar's countenance, the Sultan's pardon, and Recha's deliverance has, no doubt, a tendency to set forth a succession of natural events in the light of a miraculous ordinance, and to show therein the ways of a Divine Providence; but, unhappily, the art of the dramatic poet cannot claim for the chain of events which it forms, the same faith as for the providence of God.

Were Lessing's Nathan nothing but a family drama, and this family history the main point of the poem, the composition would be a failure in more than one respect. But the story is only the means which Lessing uses to bring out his idea, and he treats it as that idea requires, at the risk of mixing contradictory elements. In a drama proper, it is true, the plot, or, as Aristotle calls it, the "mythus," should have the first consideration. Upon this point Lessing agrees perfectly with Aristotle. He was aware of this weakness in Nathan, and therefore called it, not a drama, not a play, but "a dramatic poem."

THE CHARACTERS.

Some say that in the characters of his poem Lessing intended to represent the three religions : that in the Patriarch, Daja, the Templar, and the Laybrother he personified Christianity; in Nathan, Judaism; in Saladin, Sittah, and Al-Hafi, Islamism. There are even external objections to this view. Where does it put Recha? Al-Hafi too, with his predilection for the Parsees, and his longing for his teachers by the Ganges, is hardly a pure type of Islamism. But the internal objections are still stronger, as I shall presently prove in detail. It is

20*

absurd to suppose that Lessing meant to present us
with types of the three religions.   And this of itself
disposes of the accusation frequently made, similar
to that from which he himself had endeavored to
defend Cardanus, of his evidently having slighted
and degraded Christianity, by choosing the worst
character in the piece for its type, while Judaism
has the best.   Only a superficial reading of the
poem would so judge it.   Equally erroneous is the
idea that Lessing wished to defend and justify the
enlightened, perhaps the deistical religious views
against the orthodox.   Nathan, in that case, would
be the same in a dramatic form which Reimarus's
work was in a critical, a defence of the rational
worshippers of God.   The poem deals by no means
with definite creeds or theological doctrines.   Recha
says, " But all the more consoling was the lesson,
that our faith in God depends not on our views of
Him."

The one spring of all the characters lies deeper.
It is that which Lessing wished to set before our minds
in the story of the three rings—the difference between
true and false religion.   The true basis of religion
is self-renunciation, which enlightens the understanding in proportion as it purifies the heart, and
bears its richest fruit in that love whose source is a
right knowledge of human nature.

But in what different proportions do we find the
true mixed with the untrue, the genuine with the
counterfeit, renunciation of self with the delusions
of the imagination and the passions !   From one
side or another a shadow falls upon the light of the
soul and checks its aspirations.   Here we might
imagine a group of widely differing characters, in
which the true idea is working its way out of the

untrue, until it reaches the measure of its perfect development.

THE PATRIARCH.

In such a group of characters, the direct opposite to the truly religious should not be wanting. There is a form of selfishness which puts on the outward show of religion, with full consciousness of the mask. This is religious hypocrisy, whose prototype is Tartuffe. But there is a step below even Tartuffe;—when the egotist believes himself in all sincerity to be a man of God, and his designs to be well pleasing to God; when religion is not the mask, but the coat of mail in which egotism dwells as in a fortress—safe, comfortable, bulletproof, even beyond the reach of exposure, which, by the conscious hypocrite, is constantly dreaded and guarded against.

The type of this form is the Patriarch. Heartless to inhumanity, and so hardened against every feeling of generosity as to be utterly incapable of understanding them. he lives under the generous protection of Saladin : knows that Saladin has bestowed life and liberty upon the Templar, and yet suggests to the Templar that he should use this very liberty to become a spy upon Saladin, and his murderer. He hears of an orphan Christian child brought up by a Jew as if it were his own, but sees nothing in this tender circumstance but the robbery of a soul, and thinks that it had been better for this Jew to let the child perish.

There is no faint emotion of humanity in his soul, which he is trying to stifle in obedience to his Church. Were he only a blind instrument, his submission might be a sign of that self-renunciation which has been the strength of the Church. But there is nothing of this in him—nothing either of its humility or its pride. His own interests are uppermost with him.

He hates the Sultan, whose rule is naturally less agreeable to him than that of an orthodox king, and seeks to rid himself of it by treason and assassination. But this does not deter him from appealing to him against the Jew who has brought up a Christian child in his own faith, or perhaps in none. He is prompt to convince the Sultan of the necessity of religion in the State, and he thus makes religion itself serve him as a means to power. Yet he remains the same ready servant of any power, no matter how hateful, that may be dangerous to him. No sooner does he hear that the Templar is summoned before Saladin than he changes his tone:

> " Ah !—The Knight, I know,
> Found favor with the Sultan. I but pray
> To be remembered favorably to him."

We see that he would crawl if the Sultan stood before him.

This Patriarch has not the least vocation for martyrdom. He will take good care never to sacrifice himself. Even his intolerance and fanaticism are kept within the bounds of self-interest. His religion has agreed with him well. Lessing's few words describe him—" A red, fat, jolly prelate."

We look for characters of the type of the Patriarch not only among prelates, but wherever public ends, whether political or religious, whether those of a whole community or of a sect, are made subservient to individual interest. The type remains the same under the most various forms.

When these persons are in authority, we may be sure the Jew will go to the stake. As long as the power is with Saladin, whom they secretly hate, we may be sure of finding them in waiting with their assurances of submission—"I but pray to be re-membered favorably to him."

DAJA.

In the Patriarch, pride of faith and egotism of faith are simply pride and egotism, destitute of every sort of piety and disinterestedness. But we should be unjust to human nature did we conclude that bigotry is incapable of any nobler shape and impulse. Men do not generally make their faith; they receive it—receive it under the best and noblest influences that they can. The conviction of possessing the true faith is therefore a necessary result of religious training. From this readily arises a religious conceit, which in narrow natures amounts to bigotry and arrogance. Religion is looked upon as a piece of property to make a show of, like any worldly possession. This is doubtless a very low form of religious culture, but not an utterly false one. It has only stood still in the first infantile beginnings of religious development, where faith is without understanding. It is the ordinary, immature form of piety—true and sincere in its way, acting up to what understanding it has, and knowing no better. In such cases the heart is not lacking in good intentions as much as in that education without which the best intentions are perverted and misled.

A type of this very common form of religion is

Daja. She is actuated by two impulses—her love for Recha, to whom she clings with all fidelity and devotion, and the firm conviction, mechanically acquired, that only in *her* Church can men be saved. So her love to Recha is turned into fear for her salvation. In such a disposition unselfishness is cramped by ignorance and vanity. Out of love to Recha she wants to save her, and does not see that the separation from Nathan must break her heart. It is somewhat suspicious in so devout a Christian, that she wants to save Recha from the Jew by marrying her to the Templar. Daja's faith becomes so tolerant as to disregard the vows of a Christian Order, if she can only make a match! Her self-love is as great as her affection for Recha. This attachment furthers her own little interests. Nathan knows Daja better than she knows him. When she speaks of her conscience, Nathan says :

> " Let me but tell you first
> What stuffs in Babylon I bought for you !"

Her dearest wish is to take Recha back to Europe—to her faith, and her home. But her own interest is not forgotten. She calls out to the Templar, after having betrayed the secret of Recha's birth :

> " But when you take her back to Europe, Knight,
> Pray, leave me not behind."

So her religion, like her love, is half selfishness.

THE TEMPLAR.

Let us now substitute for bigotry a character totally free from it, regarding it as worthy of ridicule and condemnation, lifting against it the whole force of a disinterested and magnanimous heart, and a

fulness of passionate scorn. In this scorn lies a danger. Contempt of error involves pride in being free from it. This pride betrays immaturity, ignorance. Soaring above intolerance and fanaticism, in its very flight it loses itself in intolerance and fanaticism. Lessing knew the inconsistency well, and was without a trace of it himself. As Herder has excellently said, he was no freethinker, but a right-thinker. The hasty free-thinker esteems himself infinitely better than the slaves of bigotry, and despises them for the very reason that they esteem themselves. Where the spirit of free-thinking, born of a pure and noble impulse, takes the direction of pride, it finds the barrier at which the capacity for self-renunciation is checked and corrupted.

A well-drawn type of such a character is the Templar. His Order has imposed upon him chains which he writhes under and at last inwardly shakes off. The wars of religion, in which his life has been passed, have given him an experience of religious fanaticism. The spirit which has begun to spread through his Order favors his private indifference to creeds, and he expresses himself with passionate violence whenever he encounters what he takes for religious self-sufficiency. Where could this be greater than among the people which esteems itself the chosen of the Lord? Hence his fierce contempt of the Jews. The words which he ignorantly and unjustly aimed at Nathan would apply well enough to himself: "Not all who scorn their chains are free."

Yet these qualities in the Templar are so well managed, and their origin so clearly explained, that we do not expect and hardly wish them to be otherwise. The experience of his life has shown him only the dark side of the different religions, has aroused in him only a bitter hatred of bigoted conceit. He is young, and, after the manner of youth, quick to reject a thing wholly which seems to him in one respect unjust.

The Templar's is a rare nature. He has one trait in common with his poet, which, simple as it is, is seldom found. He is perfectly true ; he will seem nothing he is not. Even his mistakes are so sincere and undisguised that they soon yield to fuller knowledge. If we set aside the bonds of faith imposed by his Order, which, after all, have not fettered him much, we shall find the white mantle, with its red cross, an appropriate badge for him. The noble traits which constituted the power of the Order are in harmony with his personal inclinations—heroism, contempt of death, renunciation of the world. In these he is a true Templar.

His early renunciation of the world makes him abandon himself to solitude, resent every intrusive approach, feel a weariness of life creeping over him, and a disposition to sadness in the very fulness of his youth. Misanthropy, as a principle, is never just, and proves itself false by being always linked with an exaggerated self-consciousness, and the involuntary satisfaction it occasions is of the nature of egotism. A misanthropy acquired so early in life as the Templar's has too little knowledge of men. Its judgments are harsh, and applied by wholesale. He reasons thus : They are all egotists, even in their religion, where they should be least so ; and the Jews are the worst, because their religion obliges them to be egotists ; they first started this finding fault with others, first called themselves the chosen people, first had the arrogance to set up

their God as the only true God. And the next step
is—"Each Jew is like all Jews."

Nathan, however, reads the Templar's heart, and
recognizes the magnanimity capable of self-sacrifice,
darkened by a pride amounting almost to self-exal-
tation. He gradually removes the barrier between
them, and the two recognize in one another the
same aspirations of an enlightened, unshackled
humanity.

THE LAY-BROTHER.

The unselfishness of the Templar is crippled by
scorn of the world and mankind. He inwardly
revolts against the bigotry that he sees dominant in
the religions of the world : this leads to misanthropy, misanthropy to pride, and pride to that
glorification of self which is inconsistent with self-
renunciation. Take from self-renunciation this
limitation which oppresses and obscures it, substitute for self-glorification its extreme opposite—self-
depreciation—and you have a character of the humblest sort ; one of those insignificant natures which
cannot make themselves insignificant enough—
which prefer to live away from men, or, if among
men, to be always obedient and submissive. Our
poem furnishes us with this necessary type in the
Lay-brother. Too gentle to hate those who differed
from him, and too peaceable to lead the wild life
of a soldier, he became a hermit. Now he is a friar
at Jerusalem, and must be obedient to the Patriarch's
orders. He will become a tool of the basest curiosity,
a spy, if he allows himself to be used so. Obedient
and submissive he certainly is, but not so blind nor

so simple as the Patriarch supposes. He knows enough of human nature to see through the Patriarch, and is too pure to serve his evil purposes, too cunning to be as cunning as he would have him.

In his religion, compassion and love, as well as submission, are all-important. So far he is a true Christian. The conversation with Nathan, when he warns him of the spying tricks of the Patriarch, admirably expresses the character. Had the Jew taken compassion on the Christian child, been a loving father to the orphan, only to fall a victim to the Inquisitor? The simply human and truly pious mind of the Brother cannot frame the thought.

The Patriarch and the Lay-brother—one of the highest dignitaries of the Church, and one of the humblest of the laity ! The question to be decided is the fate of a child. The prelate would have the child perish in misery rather than be saved by a Jew. The Brother only thinks—"Children need love."

The Lay-brother and the Templar both hostile to religious fanaticism ! How much wiser the Brother in his simple piety than the Templar in his proud independence ! The Templar sees in the Jew only the self-sufficiency of his creed ; the Brother sees in the Christian's hate of the Jews, only hate.

> " It oft has vexed,
> Provoked me, e'en to tears, to see how Christians
> Forget our Saviour was himself a Jew."

The Lay-brother and Nathan—the Christian and the Jew ! When Nathan tells him at what a moment he received the Christian child, how his wife and seven sons had just been slain by the Christians, how he had taken the child, kissed it, thanked God for it—"Of seven, Thou grantest me one again !" —the Brother exclaims :

" You are a Christian, Nathan ! Yes, by heaven,
You are a Christian ! Never was a better !"

And Nathan answers :

" What makes of me a Christian in your eyes,
Makes you in mine a Jew.—Happy for both !"

Yet, genuine as the piety of the Lay-brother is, there is something ignoble in it. He is fleeing from the world—he fears its contact. He is at ease only when free from the cares and duties involved in association with men. He feels insecure amidst human activity, where the best deed may have fatal consequences. The good and the evil are so closely woven together, that the two can hardly be distinguished. To avoid the evil, he must beware even of the good. But is there any good to be found without this dangerous neighborhood? Renunciation of the world is less than overcoming the world.

THE DERVISE.

It is difficult to find the happy mean in renunciation of the world ! In the Templar it is joined to pride and passion ; in the Lay-brother, to humility, which degenerates into pusillanimity. It makes the Templar bitter, the friar powerless.

There is a renunciation of the world, which is cramped by no such limitations, perfectly unartificial and unconstrained, in which the soul is conscious of its full power and the blessedness of freedom. This form of it is native to the East. Its successful type in our poem is the dervise, Al-Hafi. There is nothing in the world to fetter the dervise ; no passion ensnares him, no good allures him, no master keeps him in dependence. He possesses

nothing, and wants nothing. His is the poverty
of a beggar and the independence of a king. What
worked upon this beggar to forsake his contempla-
tive life and become the comptroller of Saladin's
wealth ? Was he avaricious, or did the Sultan discover in the dervise an undeveloped financier?
Neither. Saladin wanted only the dervise, the man
who has the virtue of not wanting anything and not
having anything ; he wanted the beggar who would
be tender of the poor, and give free play to the
royal generosity. And these generous motives satisfied the dervise. But Al-Hafi is too clear-sighted to
be long deceived by an ideal. He soon makes the
discovery that the management of the public treasure
requires other qualities than the generosity of the
king and the humanity of the treasurer ; that the
best dispositions of the heart are poor agents where
the public weal is concerned ; that this benevolent
ideal is perverted into folly and confusion when the
public treasure is dissipated in gifts and charities.
The benevolent and generous king is in danger of
becoming a plague upon mankind, and finally a
prey to the covetous. "When princes are the vultures amidst the carrion, it is bad enough ; but
when they are the carrion amidst the vultures, 'tis
ten times worse !"
     The dervise sees the folly into which Saladin is un-
consciously leading him. This knowledge makes
him dissatisfied with himself. " O fool ! The fool
too of a fool !" He must condemn the folly ; must
give the thing its right name ; must atone for his
self-deception by the frankest acknowledgment of it.
And yet in Saladin's lavishness is a magnanimity to
which Al-Hafi feels himself akin. He cannot help
tracing out the good side of this foolery, as he calls

It, and he is vexed with himself again for doing so—for secretly loving the folly he must abandon. Our dervise's head and heart are at open variance. Before he took the post of treasurer they were in perfect sympathy. He longs to be once more the dervise who was nothing but a dervise.

He is not suited for the court. The one only pleasure in which he takes passionate delight— playing chess—is made distasteful to him. Saladin loses enormous sums to Sittah. That would be no great harm, for Sittah economizes them, and the Sultan's lost games are the one secret bit of profitable finance carried on at court. But not only does Sittah pretend to win money ; she even pretends to win the game itself. All make-believe ! Generosity, and benevolence, and chess ! Such things are not to be borne by the dervise, with his horror of all the world's delusion. Out of tune and temper he is already ; at enmity with himself, and will be an enemy of his race if he do not return betimes to his free element. In a moment he is up and away. He takes leave of none but Nathan. He would prefer to take him as the companion of his philosophic solitude. But even in the dervise's renunciation of the world is a want which crippled it, and makes it barren of all true force and freedom.

True self-abnegation overcomes the world, is not estranged from it. The Templar, the friar, and the dervise, unlike as they are, resemble one another in this—that they do not stand the test of true renunciation of the world. The Templar likes to feel melancholy. "Woman, do not make these palms, 'neath which I've loved to walk, grow hateful to me," he says to Daja. A hundred times a day the friar wishes himself on Tabor. And the dervise longingly exclaims, "Beside the Ganges only are there men."

Here is renunciation of the world consisting in flight from it. In such a case, human love works in just the opposite way from the force of attraction in the material world : attraction diminishes as the distance increases, while this form of human love increases with the distance. It is not free except in the wilderness. Among men, where its proper field should be, it is so out of time that it might easily grow into its opposite. This is what the experienced Nathan fears for his friend :

> " Al-Hafi, make all haste
> To get into your wilderness again.
> I fear lest, living among men, you'll cease
> To be a man yourself."

SALADIN AND SITTAH.

We will now contemplate unselfishness in high places, above the range of ordinary human activities.

In Saladin, we have unselfishness in its greatness, cramped by no limitations. At the height of power, he is simple and content. The whole force of unaffected, unconstrained self-conquest makes the freedom and the strength of his soul. Hence his ability to govern men.

There is nothing paltry in this great soul. His mind is open and receptive of all human greatness. Nobility, wherever found, he joyfully welcomes as akin to himself—the dervise's disinterestedness, Nathan's wisdom, Richard's heroism. There is no dividing wall between the king and the beggar, the Mussulman and the Jew, the chivalrous Sultan and the chivalrous King.

A mind so susceptible to true humanity, wherever found, easily rises above prejudices and narrow judgments. He looks men through, and therefore need neither fear nor shun them. He lets every one take his own way. To foster and develop good in all its forms is a necessity to him, his vocation. There is something of Haroun al Raschid in our Sultan. The generous-minded Saladin, with his toleration of all forms of life and forms of faith, would never of himself have thought of putting to Nathan the trying question : "Which is the true religion?" Such a question is not at all like him, certainly not the using it as a snare to entrap the Jew. It was well conceived by Lessing to make this trick originate with Sittah instead of Saladin.

The Sultan, in the Italian story, did not care for the truth, but only for the captious question which was to ensnare the Jew. He is curious to see how the Jew will escape. He therefore was satisfied by a skilful evasion. Not so the Sultan of our poem, who sought truth itself, and was eager for the solution of the great, human question. In a single word, Nathan explains the natural spring of faith, the same in all religions : "Why should I not believe my fathers just as firmly as you yours?" Religious faith is intimately connected with domestic love—the altar with the hearth. This sinks into Saladin's soul. He is, of all men, most loving of his own. His faith is the faith of his fathers. This obstinate and illiberal adherence of each to his own faith brings the religions into conflict, sows discord among the sons with their rings, and finally brings them before the judge. Such is the condition of the world in which Saladin lives, himself a soldier for the faith of his fathers. This is the point he

wants Nathan to arrive at in his story.   His expec-
tation strained to the utmost, he impatiently inter-
rupts him :

> "And now the judge ?
> I long to hear what words you give the judge.
> Go on !"

He hears what his enlightened mind quickly and
joyfully understands.   The contest between the
religions lets loose all the passions, which com-
pletely obscure all that is genuine in religion.   So
long as the sons stand up each for his own right
with mutual hatred, all these rings are false.   "The
genuine ring was lost."   "Oh, excellent !" cries
Saladin.

When the modest judge gives his counsel instead
of a sentence—Let every one believe his ring the
true one, prove the power of the stone in his ring,
awaken the love of others by his love, then will the
day of reconciliation come, and with it the wiser
judge, who has no further need to be a judge—
light breaks in upon the Sultan.

Nathan feels he is understood.   He speaks directly to Saladin—

> "If, therefore, Saladin, you feel yourself
> That promised, wiser man—"

And here we see the true effect of the story on
Saladin.   He is not intoxicated by this view of the
great tendency of the age, or by the task which
claims him ; he sees only how far he and his age
are from the goal ; feels but his own insignificance
in comparison with it :

> "I ? Dust !—I ? Naught !
>
> O God !
>
> Nathan, Nathan !
> Not ended are the thousand, thousand years
> Your judge foretold ; not mine to claim his seat.
> Go, go !—But be my friend."

This scene between Saladin and Nathan has become a pattern which has provoked the imitation
of dramatic poets—this idea of bringing the ruler
of the world and the world's wise man face to face.
The greatest imitation is the famous scene between
Philip and Posa, in Schiller's *Don Carlos*—between
the despot of the world and the citizen of the world.
I give the scene in Nathan the preference. The
greater the difference in the nature of the two characters, the more skill and imagination is displayed
in their meeting. With the simplest means Lessing
gradually produces the greatest effects ; and when
the sympathy ,between Nathan and Saladin finally
reveals itself, and is cemented into friendship, we
see what lay at the foundation of both characters.
It is this that makes the effect of the whole so
genuine and irresistible. How excellently Lessing
has introduced the dialogue ! The Sultan, throwing
out his question at first as on the spur of the moment, with a sovereign's caprice, a royal dilettan-
tism, requiring not only a direct answer to this
most difficult and embarrassing of questions, but
requiring it at once, as quick as possible :

> "Speak—
> Your answer ! Or a moment would you have
> To think upon it ? Good ; I grant it you.
> But quick, be quick with your reflections."

In every word a Sultan ! And now, impressed
by the significance of the question, as Nathan goes
on with his story until, at last, all the Sultan disap-
pears, and he cries out : " I ? Dust !—I ? Naught !"

This scene underwent a singular test, when, in
March, 1842, a Greek translation of Lessing's Na-
than was acted in Constantinople before Greeks and
Turks. The Turks were at first amazed that the

Jew should be so much at ease with the Sultan.
But at the story of the three rings they broke out
into shouts of applause.

In Saladin, everything is on a large scale. Sittah
loves him as only a sister can love such a brother.
Her soul is fashioned after this pattern, and the
kindred traits are unmistakable in the sister. But
nature has diminished them into womanly proportions, and made of Sittah not only a repetition, but
a supplement of Saladin. In his grand mode of
thinking and feeling, Saladin is apt to overlook
trifles. Just in these trifles does Sittah show more
clear-sightedness, more knowledge of the world,
more tact. Saladin cannot escape being deceived,
embarrassed. Sittah is less often misled. Her
precautions, her judgment, are helpful in anticipat-
ing and relieving her brother. So in little things
she exercises a kind of authority over Saladin, to
which he willingly submits. The alliance with
Richard was a favorite scheme of Saladin. Sittah
has always laughed at his sanguine dreams. She
knows more of the Christians and their pride. Her
glance is keener for such things than Saladin's, and
her spirit less noble in bearing them. She is bitter
against that pride of religion. He counts it among
things petty enough to be overlooked.

Sittah's character is by no means as simple as
Saladin's. She is actuated by a multitude of almost
imperceptible feminine motives. While accomplish-
ing one noble purpose, she manages to gratify
numerous minor interests. In this lies her cunning ; and she is never quite satisfied unless she can
employ cunning, as is illustrated in her preparation
for Saladin's interview with Nathan.

Looking at the noble side of Saladin's character,

we have failed to note the imperfections which must
be found in even so great a nature :—not those
universal imperfections which belong to the limitations of humanity, but such as are peculiar to
characters of this sort—natural ingredients of this
kind of greatness.

He has won for himself the sovereign control.
His powers and his destiny are in perfect harmony.
He can follow his inclinations freely, without inves-
tigating them too closely. His native greatness of ˙
mind leads him into the path of greatness. Hence
his disinterestedness; it has no deeper source.
Saladin could hardly resolve to do anything contrary to his natural inclinations. Here ends his
unselfishness. Generosity is his inclination, his
passion. To check this passion would be to conquer himself. A wise economy in his case would
be a test of earnest self-sacrifice. He does not stand
the test. He is lavish because he cannot help it.

Before his conversation with Nathan, the Sultan is
not conscious of any reasons for his tolerance, and
seems never to have raised the question of the in-
ward worth of religion. When he says, "Let me
hear the reasons which I have not myself the time
to find," he is in earnest in wanting them ; at the
same time the question betrays the most immature
conceptions of the source and nature of human
belief. When Nathan, in his story, makes true
toleration rest upon deep religious experience, the
Sultan would not have been so much startled had
the truth not been a new one to him.

What is wanting in this Saladin, and always must
be wanting in characters like his, is depth of insight,
reflection, wisdom. A nature that rests only on
inclinations, however noble, is never sure of not

being at moments false to itself. This Sultan m₄y have had his fits of despotism, his outbreaks of violence, when passion mastered him. Nothing saved the Templar from Saladin's vengeance but his resemblance to Saladin's brother. Of himself he says : "I too, alas ! have many sides, which seem hard to reconcile."

NATHAN AND RECHA.

It is indispensable to the firm establishment of unselfishness and love of humanity that they should rest, not on transient emotions, but on true wisdom and experience. Disinterestedness becomes an actual virtue only when knowledge of the world guards it from becoming misanthropy, and when wisdom shields it from the illusions of passion. So we rise to the height of our poem. One character stands before us, to which the others are but stepping-stones. Whatever of truth is found in the Templar's self-devotion and liberality of spirit, in the friar's humility, in the dervise's unselfishness and asceticism, in Saladin's generosity and magnanimity, is all united in Nathan under the control of experience and wisdom.

The only character in the poem with whom Nathan has nothing in common is the Patriarch. Even Daja, looking down upon the Jew in her pride of Christianity, must admire him : "Who doubts that Nathan is honor, generosity itself?" All the others feel the bond of a common humanity, and are irresistibly attracted towards him. "We must be friends," says the Templar. "Be my friend !" pleads Saladin. "You are a Christian,

Nathan ! Yes, by heaven ! you are a Christian !"
cries the friar. He is the only one Al-Hafi wants
to take with him to the Ganges.

This Nathan possesses the power of the original
ring, the art of winning hearts. He knows men ;
and because he knows them, he can be patient with
them. Narrowness comes from ignorance. To
purify men, is to educate them. How can they
be educated without dealing with each one according to his own nature, without changing ignorance
into a need and a capacity ? Lessing understood
religion to be the education of the human race, and
from this idea, the last he bequeathed to us, he explains the historical necessity of different forms of
revelation and belief.

A type of religion, in this sense, is his Nathan.
In him, toleration is not a mere matter of inclination and personal gratification, but of determination,
character, moral training. Such a training is the
ripest fruit of a mature experience. In every word
and act of Nathan, we trace this impress of perfect
maturity. His judgments are drawn from the fulness of experience ; his sentences are truths that he
has lived : they flow from his heart, simple, natural,
sure. He has made himself what he is. He has
fought the fight of self-abnegation, and its hardest
battles are behind him. He has been purified by
trials. The Christians had slain his wife and sons :
he took his revenge by becoming a father to a
Christian child, and never spoke of his deed.

Here we read his character. His self-sacrifice is his
resolution. After this trial there need be no second.
His will is not in sympathy with inclination ; it is
not natural nobility, like Saladin's, but moral. His
self-sacrifice has cast off all that is unreal ; it stum-

22

bles not at pride or fear; it strays neither into misanthropy nor asceticism.   He who has been brought so near to hatred of a creed, will not arrogantly condemn hatred of a creed in others.   He who has so wrestled with himself and his passions, can make allowance for passions in others : the less he has yielded to his own, the more allowance he will make.   Such self-conquest is the purest source of human knowledge and of love in the wide sense.

But why did Lessing make Nathan a Jew?

That question is always asked, and often in a tone of blame.   " The Patriarch a Christian—and Nathan a Jew!" people exclaim.   " In the Patriarch, Lessing has gratified his hatred of Christianity ; in Nathan, his predilection for Judaism.   In the Patriarch, he was representing his enemy, the Pastor Götze ; in Nathan, his friend the Jewish philosopher, Moses Mendelssohn."   And so the choice of these characters is accounted for by the prejudices of the poet, who, it is claimed, was in sympathy with everything hostile to Christianity.   So must judgments err which start from the idea that the three religions are personified in the poem.

Why is Nathan a Jew?   To answer this question aright, we need consider neither Lessing's friendship for Mendelssohn, nor the reaction of that time in favor of Judaism.   We only need to understand the character as the poem presents it—a character in which toleration springs from self-renunciation, and is the result of an effort.   It is easy to be tolerant where there is no reason for being otherwise. The *virtue* of toleration is not easy—it must spring from conflicts.

Take, now, a religion by nature intolerant and

proud, the proudest, the most oppressed of all the religions of the world. Imagine a man permitted by his religion to esteem himself the chosen of God, but condemned by the world, despised and rejected of men. If his soul yields to this twofold pressure, and follows the natural course of human passions, it must be consumed by hatred and revenge. There must be kindled a thirst for vengeance, so demoniacal, so beastly in beastly natures, that it would tear the pound of flesh from an enemy's heart, if only to bait a hook with it. Yet when these passions, which in their worst and lowest forms make a Shylock, are conquered by a noble soul—when toleration is wrested from a religion at once the proudest and most oppressed—we have a Nathan. He will not now, indeed, narrowly represent his religion; but toleration would not cost what it does, if he did not prize his religion and were not in sympathy with it. He still feels it to be his religion, the faith of his people and his fathers—the faith to which he is linked by a thousand indissoluble ties. He does not represent Judaism, but he is and remains a Jew—not because Judaism is a tolerant religion, but because it is the reverse. Who that understands his character would wish him otherwise? The admiring expression of the Templar describes him—"What a Jew! Who yet insists on seeming wholly, only Jew!"

Lessing wished to depict self-renunciation under the most unfavorable conditions, and self-seeking under the most favorable. Where faith appears but as the tool of ambition, every religion, as such, is too good to be represented. A character like the Patriarch represents not religion, but egotism intrenched behind religion. Such characters join

themselves to the dominant faith of their time, what
ever it may be.   They are to be met everywhere,
and we are far from making any one form of religious belief responsible for the Patriarch.

It is plain now why Lessing made his heartless
egotist the Patriarch, and Nathan a Jew.   The
characters that he wanted to represent required it.
That he should draw some qualities from the life,
should trace in the Patriarch some likeness to the
pastor of Hamburg, comes under the legitimate
province of the dramatic poet.

Let us return to Nathan.   What he has learned
by experience he wishes to give by education to the
child who is to take the place of his sons.   The
fruit of this education is Recha.   She is what Nathan
has made her.   A wise education forms our second
nature out of the capacities of the first ; it does not
destroy, but develops ; it seeks to cleanse the true
and bring it forward into action.   Thus has Nathan
educated Recha.   In her, unselfishness is second
nature, not a hardly won virtue.   What Nathan has
worked out for himself under the most unfavorable
circumstances is developed in Recha's soul under
the most favorable.   Nathan's virtue grows out of
self-conquest—out of victory over the proud and oppressed religion in which he was trained, and over
the natural desire for revenge kindled in him by a
hard fate.   Recha's virtue from the outset merely
obeys the voice of the tenderest of fathers.   She is
not brought up as a Jewess, but merely as Nathan's
daughter.   She knows Nathan only as her father,
and the world only through him.   In his hand her
soul feels safe and free ; and foreign to her are all
representations that would draw her away from him
to another religion and another home.   To every

word of Nathan's her heart involuntarily opens;
involuntarily it closes against every suggestion of
Daja. She lives in her father. In him is her
world, her religion, her home ; away from him, her
thoughts are busy with him—her imagination follows
him on his journey, her soul trembles at his possible dangers ; the thought of him gives new percep-
tions--she feels his approach, she anticipates his
return, and her soul forsakes her body to haste to
meet him.

Here we have the key-note of Recha's nature.
The impulse of self-devotion has so the force of
nature in her that it amounts to a loss of self-
consciousness. She loses herself in her longing—
hangs upon the object of it with all the strength of
a youthful, exuberant fancy—lives only for this object, exalted by her unbridled imagination above all
others. Such a devotion, amounting to the giving
up of one's own consciousness, is eccentric. In
such a condition of the mind all sober judgment of
things is changed into that excited fancy which
causes visions and dreams. Now imagine this
Recha suddenly in danger of death by fire, suddenly rescued by a stranger at a moment when all
human aid seemed hopeless. A boundless gratitude takes possession of her imagination, already
inclined to heavenly visions; her deliverance seems
to her a miracle of God, performed by the inter-
vention of a guardian angel. So to her fancy the
Templar becomes an angel. It is in the nature of
true gratitude to ennoble the benefactor. To criti-
cise a favor is a prelude to ingratitude.

Nathan sees at once the only way of purging
Recha's fancy of extravagance. How considerately
and lovingly he at first enters into her views, that

he may afterward correct them with firmness! With a father's fond flattery he first accepts her idea of an angelic apparition. "Recha would be worth an angel's visiting; and would, in him, see naught more fair than he, in her." He grants her the angel and the miracle; yet skilfully makes her accustomed to the ideas that the angel might be a man, and the miracle be wrought by natural means.

> "The greatest miracle of all is this:
> That true and genuine miracles become
> Of no significance."

This dialogue shows us again in what faith Nathan lives. For him there is but one sure test of religion—self-renunciation; and but one test of self-renunciation—the voluntary subordination of one's own will to others. All the powers within us must work together for this. The true faith, as far as it is possible in humanity, must be tested by the heart. Man cannot hold religious truth as an external possession, a philosopher's stone; it must be the very kernel of his being. "By their fruits ye  shall know them." Holding this view of religion, Nathan had never thought of putting to himself the question suddenly proposed to him by Saladin. "I pray you, tell me what belief—what law has most commended itself to you." The question takes him by surprise. It is not in his line of thought. It may be a snare, or it may be the expression of the Sultan's sincere desire for truth. In vain Nathan draws back, saying: "Sultan, I am a Jew." Saladin presses for a decisive answer. The soliloquy in which he prepares his answer is perfect in its way. None but Lessing could have written it. It should be read with a full appreciation of the fact, that Lessing's punctuation marks are significant, elo-

quent. Every comma, every semicolon speaks.
Some writers use dashes to conceal a want of
thought ; Lessing uses them when too many
thoughts crowd into one moment ; they denote that
silence which is most eloquent.

Nathan is not the traditional Jew, and does not
choose to be ; but he is and always will be a Jew.
Why ? Perhaps this simple question is raised in
his mind now for the first time. The answer is
plain. It is the faith of his people and of his
fathers, born in him with his birth, woven into all
the history of his life, a part of himself. Abandon-
ing his religion would be like abjuring his fathers.
It is his father's ring. So it is, save in characters
of exceptional strength or exceptional weakness,
with any form of belief in which one has been
brought up.

The reader has, we trust, appreciated that our
poem embodies ideas which place it beyond the requirements of merely dramatic art, and that it is
aptly called Nathan the Wise, from its fulness of
real wisdom. Surely this poem, if any, deserves to
be prefaced by the motto of the old philosopher :
" Enter here ; for here, too, are Gods."

www.ingramcontent.com/pod-product-compliance
Lightning Source LLC
Chambersburg PA
CBHW021046030726
47496CB00006B/1715